The Secret Billionaire

She doesn't know he's rich, but she's fallen for him anyway...

A complete love story, brought to you by bestselling author Vanessa Brown.

Despite Vera's full time schedule of long working hours and taking care of her mum, she knows she needs to invest in her love life.

And while signing up to an online dating service wasn't her preferred way of meeting men, it's all she had time for.

That said, it's a decisions that may just have paid off!

Soon she's matched with Archer, a handsome bachelor she just happens to have briefly met before. But what Vera doesn't know is Archer's a billionaire.

And he's desperately looking for a girl to love who is interested in him for something other than his money.

As the two spend more time together though and he breaks the news, will Vera think a great man has turned even more perfect?

Or will a relationship formed on the back of a lie be destined to fail? Find out in this sexy and secretive romance by Vanessa Brown of BWWM Club.

Suitable for over 18s only due to sex scenes so hot, you'll want to me your own secret billionaire.

Get Free Romance eBooks!

Hi there. As a special thank you for buying this book, for a limited time I want to send you some great ebooks completely **free of charge** directly to your email! You can get it by going to this page:

www.saucyromancebooks.com/physical

You can see a the cover of these books on the next page:

These ebooks are so exclusive you can't even buy them. When you download them I'll also send you updates when new books like this are available.

Again, that link is:

www.saucyromancebooks.com/physical

Contents

Chapter 1

"Shit shit shit shit!" Vera cried as she bolted out of the cab. She had already paid the cabbie and the only thing she was looking at was the gate that was in front of her. "Move aside, please!" she yelled warning people in front of her. Holding her bag in one hand and a ringing phone and purse in the other, Vera entered the airport and did not stop to take a look around. She knew where she needed to be and her feet took her to her destination.

The shiny floor was making all the efforts to make her slip, but she was used to running on this floor. This was not the first time she was running in here. "Coming through! Excuse me!" she kept yelling while running. The people in front of her were able to hear her loud and clear, and so she did not bump into anyone — though a few time she had near misses with elderly people who were not able to move just in time. Through the crowd she was now able to see the desk of *Lagoona Airlines*. A long line of passengers starting from the counter was going all the way back to the lounge. It was raining chaos over all the airport — the weather had suddenly taken a turn for worse and the flights were being delayed. Quickly, Vera ran past the long line of the passengers and ran towards the door that had 'Employees Only' written on it.

"You are late, Vera!" the woman by the gate tried to inform her as she entered. But Vera was not interested in listening to anything. Inside, she quickly took off her coat and stood before her locker. Stuffing her coat and purse inside, she quickly stood before a mirror that had bright lights and makeup placed in front of it. Vera fixed her face and hair and took a final look at her dress that was hiding under her coat earlier.

Jane was able to see Vera from the counter outside, "Vera!!" she cried peeking her head inside the tiny window.

"Coming!" Vera yelled back as she saw herself for one last time to ensure she was looking spick and span. Seconds later, she was at the counter beside Jane.

"Thank God you are finally here!" Jane was letting her know that her presence was appreciated, but Miranda was not in a good mood, "We have been dealing with this all morning. You are not supposed to be late on a day like this. Flights are getting delayed and people are going crazy."

"I get it Miranda! Now let me do my job, alright!" Vera was taking charge of the situation.

"This is bullshit!" An irate passenger yelled at Vera, "I am not booking any other flight. I paid you guys and you are supposed to fly me out of this pathetic city."

"I am sorry sir, but all the flights are being grounded due to the incoming storm." Vera was trying to be polite. Inside, she wanted to throw this guy's ticket in his face and tell him to get the fuck out of here. But she liked having this job and so decided to keep that plastic smile on her face.

"I am going to sue you guys. You just wait!" the man threatened before leaving the counter. Vera knew he was not going to do anything.

The whole staff was used to getting these idle threats all the time. Almost all of the unhappy passengers for one reason or the other, threatened to sue the airlines. "I would want at least somebody to actually do it," Jane used to say often. "That way these cheap bastards would somehow learn how to run an airline properly." Like all her colleagues, Vera knew that Lagoona Airlines was one of the cheapest in the business because they were masters in cutting corners to save costs. Misplaced luggage, bad food and mishaps with bookings were some common occurrences along with regular delays for no apparent reasons.

But today was something special. Lagoona was not the only airlines that was delayed. Every other airline was facing irate passengers who were threatening to sue them. Vera often joked with Jane that *threatening to sue* is the new trend that most people liked to follow these days.

"I will sue you!" she often imitated a passenger followed by a good laugh. "Nobody has the time." Jane always said, "Do you know what you have to do to sue somebody? First, you have to hire a lawyer, most people drop the plan right at this step. And if some people dare to go beyond, they then have to help that lawyer file tonnes of paperwork. And lets face it nobody likes to file paperwork. So of all the people who actually go ahead with the plan of suing somebody or something, only 20% actually follow through. Rest of them, just give up somewhere in the middle."

Vera trusted Jane's statistics — she was good with numbers, and facts. Little did she know that her 20% was all made up, like most of her facts.

"What happened today?" Jane asked Vera while they both handled the passengers. Though they were looking and smiling at the people in front of them, Vera and Jane had screened them out of their conversation. They were able to talk to each other while working. Jane was still waiting for the answer. Vera handled the passenger in front of her and showed her beautiful smile as the next passenger replaced the last one.

"Mom! She thought our maid stole my cellphone." Vera finally answered, "And so now we are without any domestic help."

"Again?" Jane wondered. "Didn't she accuse her of stealing your blender the other day?"

Vera nodded in agreement, "Well, this time it was the phone. And to stop her from calling 911, I had to go convince her that I had misplaced the phone somewhere inside the house."

"Where did you find it then?"

"Under her pillow cover." Vera replied, "She borrowed my phone last night to talk to her sister, and forgot to give it back. And in the morning, both of us forgot that she took the phone last night. Hence, the case of the missing phone."

"Damn, that happens to me too. I put the phone under my pillow, but then I realize that it is actually inside the cover. I try to look for the phone in the morning, but its not under the pillow." Jane said.

"I just want her to be a little responsible, so that I can be less responsible." Vera said, without looking at Jane.

"Tough luck, bro!" Jane chuckled checking the boarding pass of a passenger before her.

Vera chuckled with her friend and continued attending the passengers. It was a long line and a long day ahead of them.

*****

The airport was now looking a little calmer. People had settled in. The flights were still grounded as the storm ravaged outside. The lines had disappeared from the airline desks and now people were sprawling across the lounge, cafeteria and any corner they found big enough to stretch their legs. Amidst all this, Vera and Jane were sitting at a table in the cafeteria, having their lunch and daily chat.

"So what happened? Did you get lucky?" Vera asked sipping her coffee.

"Oh Yeah! I was lucky I did not get murdered." Jane replied.

Vera was surprised. "What happened?" she leaned in with her curiosity.

Jane started retelling the story of her last night. "So I met this guy on Facebook. I told you about him, right? The one with the green eyes and broad jaw line.."

"Yeah, the one with the red sports car." Vera said.

"Yes! So we decided to meet at this club." Jane further explained, "And we were sitting in the club, minding our business when he gets up and goes to the restroom."

Vera kept nodding to show that she was on the same page.

"And when he came back, he had a white hat that was not on him when he left." Jane's face frowned, "I asked him about the hat, and that idiot told me that he took it from the restroom."

"What?" Vera found it hard to believe, "He stole a hat, from men's room?"

"Yes, and he confessed to me straight away. But I know that he was bragging." Jane remembered his face from the last night while retelling the incident, "I told him to put it back but he was a little drunk by then. '*I am going to keep it.*' he said and ordered another round of shots."

"You stayed with him after that guy stole a hat?" Vera asked.

"Hey, I was shocked! It's not everyday that your date turns out to be a drunk compulsive thief. So I just sat there, staring at his drunk face. And I swear to God, he felt as if that hat was an award. He was touching it, adjusting it all the time."

And then Jane took a pause, "But then, a big dude came up and stood behind him. He was wearing a white jacket that matched the hat."

"Oh shit!" Vera exclaimed with joy and excitement.

"So this big dude tapped on his shoulder, and this idiot turned around with a pathetic smile and said '*What the hell is your problem?*'... Imagine that."

"Then what happened?" Vera's excitement was growing.

"The big dude was surprisingly polite. He nicely asked for his hat back, but that idiot said that it was his hat. The big guy then asked him to tell the brand of the hat if it was really his." Vera was curiously looking into Jane's eyes to tell her the rest of the story.

After a brief pause, Jane continued, "Long story short my date kept saying that the hat belonged to him and did not give even one logical answer or evidence to back up his claim. The big guy then did what I was expecting him to do in the first place — he took his hat back and started beating the shit out of that idiot."

Vera laughed a little, "How was it?"

"Brutal! Security arrived and they somehow controlled the big guy."

"No, I mean how was it for your date?" Vera made herself clear.

"Ohh that idiot was bleeding through his nose when the security kicked his ass out on the street." Jane finished.

"Did they bother you? Security, I mean."

"Well, they asked me whether I wanted to join my *friend*, but I told them that I preferred to stay inside. And so they left me."

"Wow! Some night huh?" Vera exclaimed.

"I wasn't finished!" Jane continued, "I stayed there for a couple more drinks and then decided to head back home. It was around an hour later when I got out of the club. And guess who was waiting outside for me?"

"Oh no!" Vera chuckled with surprise.

"His nose still had the dried up blood. That idiot did not even clean himself." Jane told Vera, "He saw me and started yelling, 'Hey babe! I am here,' like I was his girlfriend or something."

"Wow! Did he follow you?" Vera asked getting a little worried.

"Thank God No! Luckily I found a cab and got the hell out of there. But he kept texting me though." Jane concluded the story.

"Some night!" Vera said.

"Yup. Some night." Jane agreed before realizing she was being a little rude,

"So, tell me — how did your night go? Did you get out?"

Vera took a deep breath after finishing her coffee. She then looked at Jane and just nodded 'No'.

"Wow! Again? What happened?" Jane suddenly grew a little concerned, "Was it your mom again?"

"Oh no!" Vera instantly rectified, "She was fine. I just did not want to go out."

Jane did not seem to understand this, "Is everything alright?"

"I don't know. I remember wanting to go out and meet other people when I used to be in college, but now anxiety takes me over whenever I think of going out. I feel.." Vera hesitated for a seconds, ".. old!"

"Are you kidding me?" Jane was shocked, "How old are you? 27 if I am not wrong! Then what is wrong with you?"

"I just don't feel my age anymore. Instead I feel like one of those women who live alone with a horde of cats." Vera was not sure what was wrong with her, and so she did not know how to explain it to Jane.

"That is bullshit! You don't even like cats. Why are you so depressed?" Jane leaned in to look into Vera's eyes.

"I don't know!" Vera kind of snapped. She did not like this conversation. Jane got the hint and backed off. An awkward silence took over the table as they both looked around, waiting for this weirdness to go away.

Jane then looked at Vera, "When was the last time you bought new lingerie?"

"What kind of question is that?" Vera wondered.

"Change, you see is a great motivator. It can make us uncomfortable, but it also helps us get over our anxiety. Whenever I feel down and out," Jane looked into Vera's eyes, ".. and *old*... I go out and buy new lingerie."

"How does that help?" Vera did not understand where Jane was going with this.

"Well, when you see yourself in the mirror, dressed in that sexy lingerie .. you feel alive!"

Vera was looking at Jane without blinking her eyes. Though she was still confused how this could have helped anyone in overcoming anxiety, she wanted to know more about it.

Jane continued looking at Vera's hands, "Some white and red lacy lingerie will look gorgeous on your silky black skin. And those curls.." Jane moved her eyes to Vera's hair, "will make you look like a goddess."

"Wow! That was weird." Vera chuckled a little.

"Trust me." Jane supported her claims, "If I were a dude, I would be totally into you. Both figuratively and literally."

Vera did not know whether Jane was genuinely complimenting her or flirting with her. But all these praises gave a massage to her battered self confidence.

"I am telling you Vera. All you need is to catch up with that young girl locked deep inside you. The _real_ you!!"

"And where will I find this real me?" Vera jokingly asked.

"In the mirror, you silly!" Jane replied confidently. "All you need to do is remind yourself who you used to be... and be that girl again that you loved. Change your look, your clothes, and you will find that girl in your mirror."

Vera did not know whether she wanted to meet that girl in the mirror, but it certainly sounded tempting.

"Do it. Go home and try some old clothes that you loved." Jane said.

"Alright, I will try." Vera wanted Jane to stop now. "Come, lets go back," she said getting up. She could see that their break was over,

Together, they walked back to their desk and waited for passengers. But the rest of the evening seemed so quiet.

*****

At home, Vera was standing in front of the mirror. She was looking at her face and it seemed like she was staring at a stranger. This is not how she remembered her face. But it had been a long time since she had paid close attention to her looks. And then she remembered Jane's words, "Change your look, your clothes, and you will find that girl in your mirror."

"Alright, here we go!" Vera said walking towards her cupboard. On the bottom shelf, she dug in behind her nightwear and found a green silk bag. Making sure not to ruin her favorite pyjamas in the front, Vera carefully pulled that green silky bag out of that forgotten corner of her cupboard.

"Lets see, what do we have here," she said opening the bag right on the floor.

With the bag, a chest of memories was opened. Vera could remember several incidents related to the dresses, tops and shorts that were in that bag. Looking at all those clothes, a warm smile appeared on her face.

Quickly, she picked up a red top and walked back to the mirror. Taking off the t shirt she was wearing, she held the top in front of her body and checked herself in the mirror. The color still looked good on her, like it used to be years ago.

Vera could see what Jane meant and so she decided to go a little further. She pulled out her set of lingerie that was piled under other clothes. She picked up a blue bra and put it on. And then she pulled out her make up kit. After a few minutes when she stepped in front of the mirror, she found the Vera she knew looking at her through the glass.

With that red top and make up, Vera was elated to see the old Vera back again. Memories of college filled Vera's brain. The parties and excursions with friends — the late night walks around the campus and having almost no care at all, it was the best time of her life. She had dreams and ambitions. But it all changed with a phone call one evening.

Vera remembered her mother's voice over the phone, "Vera, Daddy is no more," were her words. Those five words brought Vera's dreams to the ground. Her dad meant so much to her and Vera was unable to imagine her life without him. Michael Jones was the supporting pillar to his daughter and wife. Their lives revolved around this one man who was their Sun and Moon. Being the only child, Vera received all the love and care from her dad. Her mother though was still a little childish. Alice Jones had a lot of growing up to do.

After her last year at college, Vera decided to move in with her mother. Alice married Michael at a young age and gave birth to Vera when she was only 25. She was the youngest of 5 kids and in a sense never grew up. Her family never pushed her to stand on her own feet. Instead, they always helped her like the little child she was to them. When Jones were going through hard times, Alice occasionally went to her family to get 'help' behind Michael's back. Michael did find out about his wife's secret source of income, but he never said anything. The bad times soon were over and Michael assured Alice that he would one day take her around the world. It was a promise he made before they got married. But raising a kid was not cheap.

Michael showed his willingness to fulfill his promise by keeping a secret stash of money. He kept putting some of his savings in that box. "This is for our world tour," he told Alice giving her the box. "Don't you spend anything from this. Cause if you do, our agreement is void." Michael was not a lawyer, but he certainly was a smart man.

Alice kept the box in her wardrobe and dropped some money in it herself from time to time. But before the Jones could count how much they had in the box, Michael left the world. Alice forgot about the box and it stayed where it was.

Vera had been living with her mother since Michael's death. She knew her mother was not capable of taking care of herself. And there was no way she was putting her mother in a home. "You don't put your parents in a home." Vera clearly remembered her dad's words. "Parents take care of their children when they are difficult to handle, and so it's the duty of all children to return the favor when their parents are old."

Vera remembered her grandpa who lived with them until his death. And Vera knew her father walked the talk. Not only his own, but Michael Jones also cared for Alice's old parents when they needed help. He visited them every week and refilled their kitchen and refrigerator. Alice could not have ask for more from her husband.

Though her mother was not that old, Vera had decided that she was not going to let her go. "But what after you get married?" Jane had asked her several times, but Vera had no idea what she was going to do. And maybe this was the reason why she had not pursued any romantic endeavors. She did not want to delve into her psychology behind her issues. Not facing her problems made her comfortable and happy.

But today, she was looking at her past through the mirror. The Vera who had dreams of a beautiful future was staring at her.

"That looks really good on you!" Alice was looking at her from the slightly opened door.

"Mom!" Vera was shocked and embarrassed at the same time. "You are supposed to knock!"

"The door was open." Alice said coming inside the room. She went through the pile of clothes on the floor and picked up a blue dress. "Why did you stop wearing these clothes? This one looked so good on you."

Vera walked to her mother and took the dress from her hands, "I don't wear these because I wear my uniform to work. And I don't go out much now."

"Why not? You are young, you should go out more often. How else are you supposed to meet a nice guy?"

"Mom, I am focusing more on work right now." Vera tried to defend herself.

"Oh yeah. Even I know this is a dead end job." Alice was quite blunt. And then she realized this was the only thing her daughter had right now. Vera was hurt inside, but she tried really hard to not show it.

"I am sorry. You know I did not mean it that way." Alice apologized. "I just want you to enjoy your life."

Vera started putting her clothes back in the silk bag, "Mom, we have talked about this so many times." She did not want to look at her mother after her last comment about her job.

"Don't be mad!" Alice knew how Vera behaved when she was angry. "I said I am sorry. I am worried about you."

Vera could hear a sob in that last sentence, and she knew what her mother was going to do next. As she turned around and looked at her, Vera found her mother's teary eyes.

"I never wanted to be a burden on you, or anybody." Alice wiped her tears.

"Mom!" Vera dropped the clothes on the floor and took her mother to her bed. After sitting her down, Vera kneeled down in front of her and held her hands, "You are not a burden on me. And will never be."

Alice looked at her daughter after cleaning her eyes.

"This is just a phase. I guess." Vera was trying to come up with excuses for her almost dead social life. "You know I am planning to switch my job."

"I know. You had always wanted to go on adventures. But even then, I am holding you back."

"No! It's nothing like that Mom." Vera explained. "I don't want to do that anymore. All I want now is a better job with growth prospects."

Alice could tell when her daughter was lying to her, and all the signs were present on Vera's face right now. But she was trying to cheer her up so hard, that Alice did not call Vera out on her lies. Instead, she listened to her with love and patience.

"As soon as I find another job, I am leaving this one. I will have a better pay and career graph." Vera was quite confident with her lie. Maybe because she had told this lie to herself so many times that it seemed like a sure thing to her.

"Remember, Vera," Alice reminded her. "You are not bound by my responsibilities. You deserve a good future with someone you love. Don't hold yourself back, just because of me."

Vera looked down to the floor and then looked at her mother. Their was a big smile on her face, "I won't Mom. I am telling you. The moment I will find a good guy, I am going to jump on him."

This made Alice chuckled and suddenly, both of them forgot everything else. They shared some more jokes and good memories from their past, and enjoyed some quality time together in Vera's room.

Chapter 2

The ocean sprawled in all the directions with the moon showering it with its bright light. The water moved with each breeze, creating a tiny wave. There was nothing to hear, not a sound known to human ear.

"Did you feel it?" Archer Finch — 29 year old tall man with broad shoulders and blue eyes, walked behind his lovely companion.

"I think I do." Reggie, a 23 year old gorgeous model, kept looking at the ocean while drinking from her glass of wine. She picked up the bottle to pour some more into her glass.

Archer's golden hair seemed silver in the full moon light. His broad shoulders supported the beautiful embroidered shirt that fluttered with the wind. He stood really close to Reggie and looked around them — "It's haunting isn't it?" he asked. Archer and Reggie were standing in the middle of the ocean on a beautiful yacht, owned by him.

"Haunting? I think it's awesome!" Reggie said.

"Of course, it's awesome. But look at it carefully." Archer explained. "If you were on a raft made out of planks and bamboo right now, instead of this yacht. Would it still seem beautiful to you?"

And suddenly, Reggie's eyes grew wide. She gulped all her wine in one go and picked up the bottle for another refill. "Damn, we are out." Reggie said looking at the empty bottle.

She then turned to Archer who was still staring at the open sea, "You just killed my buzz with that idea. Why would anybody want to imagine themselves on a bamboo raft when they are on a million dollar yacht?"

Archer pressed a beeper on the table and took the empty bottle from Reggie, "Because life is not just about pretty and shiny things. Sometimes you need to know how brutal it can be. And what can be more brutal than this unforgiving sea?"

"Yes, Mr Finch?" an obedient voice came out of the speaker in the beeper.

Archer pressed the *speak* button, "We need a bottle of wine on the deck here."

"Sure, Mr Finch!" the voice replied.

"You are one of the richest people on earth. You don't need to worry about these kinds of things? Shouldn't you be thinking about where to spend your holidays and what to wear?" Reggie was eagerly waiting for the new wine bottle to arrive.

"The only thing I worry about beside my business, is what I am doing with my life." Archer replied, "As I just said, life is not just about pretty and shiny things. It;s much deeper than that."

An attendant arrived on deck with a wine bottle. He opened the bottle in front of Archer and placed it in the ice box. "There you go Mr Finch. Anything else?" he asked picking up the empty bottle.

"That will be all, Alex. Thank you!" Archer smiled at the young man.

Alex smiled and left with the empty bottle.

"Are all billionaires like you?" Reggie quickly filled her glass.

"Are all the other *Victoria's Secret* models like you?" Archer countered her question. "Tell me."

Reggie chuckled, "I get it. You are special." She took a big sip from her glass and then looked eagerly in Archer's eyes. "Tell me where are we going to spend this weekend?"

"I have not decided yet." Archer replied.

"Really? You took me out for this boat ride and you still don't know where we are going?"

"Alright, where do you want to go?" Archer asked with a smile.

"Somewhere warm. Like a beach. Where we can stay in a beautiful room that opens right onto the beach. There should be a kickass bar there and we will get drunk the whole day." Reggie replied, closing her eyes.

"Wow! Seems like you have figured it all out." Archer sat down.

Reggie smiled closing her eyes. She seemed quite proud of her plan. "Oh yes. I have my whole life planned ahead of me."

"Is that so?" Archer looked at her with surprise.

"Yes, I am going to continue modeling for a few more years, and then I will launch my own clothing line." Reggie unfolded her life plans before Archer while filling her glass with more wine.

Archer wanted to warn her about her excessive alcohol consumption, but he was finding Reggie more entertaining when she was drunk. When she was sober, she behaved like any typical model, putting up a facade of elegance and sensibility. But she was showing her real self after getting some wine in her. Archer was really enjoying getting to know this person. Though it was quite clear she was not her type. He was just enjoying her company for the moment they were together on this trip.

Reggie finished her glass while babbling about her clothing line from the future. She also told Archer about how petty her fellow models were. "They are just jealous because I am better looking." And soon, Archer was getting bored. This girl was turning into every drunk girl who had been with him only to enjoy the fine wine and expensive things.

"So, do you want to call it a night? We will be on a beach tomorrow." Archer politely tried to stop Reggie's binge drinking.

Reggie looked at Archer, and all the wine inside her stomach was now showing its magic. Archer's handsome face was making her body parts tingle and slowly she stood up. Archer noticed how she was fumbling while getting up.

"Are you alright?" he asked.

"Better than ever!" Reggie said as she sat over Archer. She then held his face with both her hands and kissed him. "You are so fucking hot!" She pulled her face back only to declare this and went back to kissing him.

"After we get on that beach, I am going to fuck your brains out." Reggie told Archer about her plans. Right then, she felt something vibrating in Archer's pants.

"Ooh!" she chuckled.

"It's my phone." Archer explained while gently pushing her away. He then took his phone out of his pocket. "I am sorry, I need to take this," he said getting off his chair.

Reggie stood up and as Archer walked away, she fell in his chair, "Come back soon. I am horny!" she yelled.

Archer quickly went inside the cabin and closed the door. After he made sure Reggie was not able to hear him, he answered the call, "This is not going well."

"What happened?" The voice on the other end of the phone inquired. It was Phillip Sanchez, Archer's trusted advisor and friend.

"You said this girl was different from the others." Archer said looking at Reggie from the glass window.

"Yeah, she has a degree in philosophy. I guess." Phillip replied.

"I don't think so. Because all she could think of is going to a beach, getting drunk and having sex with me."

"How is that bad?" Phillip wondered.

Archer started walking inside the cabin. He opened the door that led to the corridor and walked towards his room. "If I wanted to have sex with a beautiful woman, there was no need for me to come here, to the middle of the ocean."

"But, you are already there..." Phillip suggested. "So what is the harm in bumping a quick ugly and come back?"

"Now you are talking just like her." Archer opened the door to his room. Inside, he took off his shoes and crashed in his bed. "Hold on for a second."

He then pressed the intercom by his bed.

"Yes, Mr Finch!" Alex's voice poured through the speakers.

"Alex, I am in my room, but my friend is still on the deck. Would you be so kind and look after her. If she needs anything?" Archer politely told Alex what to do.

"Certainly Mr Finch. And what should I say if your friend asks for you?"

"Tell her I am on a conference call." Archer gave him the answer.

"Very well Mr Finch. Do you need anything in your room?" Alex asked in his never changing polite tone.

"No thanks Alex, I am fine."

"Alright Mr Finch."

"You are leaving a hot drunk girl on the deck of your yacht, while you sit in your room, talking to a guy…" Phillip recapped the situation for Archer. "Give me one good reason why somebody won't assume you are gay?"

"Maybe you are confusing me with somebody who cares about what other people think of him." Archer smiled. "How does it matter if I am straight or gay? I have a hot drunk girl on my deck who wants me."

"You just used my argument against me." Phillip said.

"Well, you always tell me I could be a good lawyer, remember?" Archer chuckled. "Besides I don't have sex with drunk girls. Right now she wants me because I own this yacht and the expensive wine she is chugging down."

"You are good looking too. Don't forget that." Phillip reminded him.

"By that logic, every good looking guy should be sleeping with a Victoria's secret model."

"I don't believe it. Do you know how many guys would kill to be in your spot right now?" Phillip almost cried.

"Why are you talking like her? You know I am not looking for _this_. I came out on this date because you said this girl was different. You wanted to play matchmaker, and now I am stuck with a drunk girl who I quote, wants to fuck my brains out."

"You say this like it's a bad thing."

"Trust me, where I am right now in my life, I am really tired of this shit." Archer said. "Every girl I meet is interested in me only because I have shit load of money."

"Again, you say this like it's a bad thing." Phillip was not able to understand why Archer was getting so mad at this.

"Listen to me, I have told you many times, and I am telling this to you again." Archer spoke very slowly. "I want somebody to love me for who I really am. And not for my money!"

There was complete silence on the phone for a few seconds.

"Did you understand what I just said?" Archer confirmed breaking the silence.

"I get it." Phillip replied, "You want a girl who should love you for who you really are.. but the problem is, you *are* a billion-aire, and that is why so many girls love you."

"Damn it Phillip!" Archer cried in frustration.

"Hey, don't yell at me my friend, it's Catch 22." Phillip replied.

"No, it's not. This is not what Catch 22 is." Archer said, "Or maybe it is. I don't know."

Phillip did not say anything. He knew his friend was getting frustrated. And so he came up with an idea, "You know what? Fuck that girl."

"No, I won't!" Archer replied assertively.

"No, I mean fuck her like.. you know.. _fuck her_.. like let her go." Phillip explained the real sentiment behind his phrasing, "We don't need her. You come back here and we will watch some movies and chill. How does that sound?"

"Pretty gay!" Archer replied.

"Well, if you don't like my plan, I suggest you stay with her." Phillip said.

"Fuck it! I am coming back. Send me a ride." Archer was feeling relieved now.

"Fuck yeah! I am sending your ride. Should be there in fifteen minutes."

"Alright, see you at the house." Archer said.

"Cool!" Phillip hung up.

Archer quickly put on his shoes and jacket. He pressed the intercom again, "Alex, I am going home."

"Alright Mr Finch. Shall I wake up your friend?"

"No need. You take her to any beach or island.. she wants to go and bring her back. I promised her a holiday." Archer did not want to ruin Reggie's plans.

"Anything else Mr Finch?"

"Just make me a tuna sandwich. I am feeling a little hungry."

"Definitely Mr Finch." Alex's voice had a warmth this time.

Archer quickly checked his phone while releasing the intercom button.

*****

Reggie was passed out in the chair when she heard a loud sound coming right at her from the sky. "What the fuck!" she almost fell on the deck. Collecting herself, she looked in the direction of a sound and saw a small airplane coming towards the yacht.

As she looked, the plane landed a few meters away from the yacht. She could see that the plane had pontoons at the bottom and now it was moving like a boat floating on the water. She walked towards the edge of the deck and could see a small boat being lowered at the back of the yacht.

"Archer?" she cried as she noticed Archer in that boat. Archer heard his name and waved at her. "Where are you going?" she yelled.

"Some urgent business needed his physical presence, I am afraid Miss."

Reggie turned around and saw Alex standing there with another bottle of wine. "Mr Finch has asked me to make sure you have a great holiday. He said you wanted to go to a beach. Where would you like to go then?"

Reggie had no idea where she wanted to go. She looked at Archer who was boarding the plane. "Is he eating a sandwich?" she asked looking at him while Archer closed the door of the plane. He waved goodbye to her and the plane started its approach.

"Yes, tuna. Would you like to have one, Miss?" Alex asked.

Reggie saw the plane taking off and disappearing in the night sky. After remaining still in one spot, she took the wine bottle from Alex and sat in the chair, "Yeah, bring me three of those."

"Very well, Miss." Alex walked away.

Reggie poured more wine in her glass.

*****

Archer's car entered the big gate of his gigantic house. It stopped at the porch and Archer entered the main door. The house had tall ceilings and wide walls. Though it had Spanish architecture on the outside, it looked completely modern from the inside. Big screens were everywhere and instead of curvy walls with heavy plaster work there were smooth walls with neutral colors.

Archer entered the main hall, passed through the study and arrived at a big open lawn. Walking to the other edge of the lawn he then entered the rec room where Phillip was sitting with his laptop.

"You are working?" Archer was surprised to see Phillip on his laptop. "You said we will watch movies and have fun."

"I remember what I said, I was just doing something for you." Phillip said working on the laptop.

"What? Finding me another bad date?" Archer laughed.

Phillip did not respond but kept working on the laptop. Archer crashed onto the big couch and looked around. He then checked his watch, "How long is this thing of yours going to take?"

"Just a few more minutes." Phillip replied.

"It's strange!" Archer tried to catch Phillip's attention. "You work for me, and yet I am here, waiting for you. Shouldn't it be the other way around?"

"You are going to thank me for this. Trust me!" Phillip looked at Archer. He knew his friend had just recovered from a bad mood swing and he did not want him to get frustrated again.

Archer kept looking at Phillip for some time. "Just a few more minutes." Phillip almost pleaded this time.

"Alright!" Archer got up. "I will go and change. But when I come back, I want you away from the laptop. I did not free my weekend to just sit here like an idiot."

"I hear you, buddy." Phillip said with a big smile.

"You know how I get when my plans fall apart." Archer tried to explain himself.

"I know. You come back and I will give you my complete attention!" Phillip promised.

Archer walked out of the room and Phillip heaved a sigh of relief. He then went back to working on his laptop. On his screen, he was creating Archer's profile on a dating site. Soon, the profile was 100% complete and Phillip smiled proudly at his accomplishment.

Minutes later, Archer came back into the rec room and he saw Phillip still standing before his laptop, "Still there! What did I tell you?"

"As I said, you now have my undivided attention." Phillip looked at Archer with a smile, "Now, I have to show you something."

Archer looked at Phillip's laptop and saw his profile on a dating site, "You cannot be serious! A dating site? I though we were going to forget about this whole thing. I am more than capable of finding a woman for myself."

"Just take a look at this first!" Phillip convinced Archer, "This is a new thing!"

"Alright, what is it?" Archer decided to listen to his friend for one more time.

"This, is a new dating site, called High Seas! Mostly made for rich people, like you." Phillip explained as he scrolled through the dating site.

"And why do you think it is better than the other dating sites?" Archer asked.

"Because, the girls you will meet here won't like you just for your money. This site is filled with rich people."

Archer clicked on the profiles of some girls, "Hey! This does not give any detail about these girls. How am I supposed to know them?"

Phillip replied with a smile, "This is the beauty of this website, you only get to know the person as you interact with them. So when you like a person, you like them for what they really are. Of course you can tell them who you really are, but where is the fun in that?"

"How stupid is that? Who came up with his terrible idea?" Archer was astonished to hear the concept. "Just go through it, alright?" Phillip pleaded and so Archer decided to give it a shot.

Archer browsed through the website, "So you are telling me that I can meet girls here who won't know that I am rich..?" He then looked at Phillip who nodded in a 'Yes'.

"Alright, lets give this a shot. But right now, I really want to watch a movie." Archer closed the lid of the laptop.

"Fair enough." Phillip stood straight.

"I will choose." Archer said, turning the TV on.

"Not another documentary, please! I want to see a real good drama." Phillip requested.

"What are you, a girl?"

*****

Archer started logging on High Seas and met a girl Claudia from Sweden. He really felt a connection with her and in a week he was able to see her details. Archer was relieved to know that Claudia was also immensely wealthy like him. Hitting it off online, and on phone, both of them decide to meet. "I need to be in Frankfurt for a few days. Would you like to join me there?" he asked Claudia over the phone.

"I am afraid I won't be able to. I have to spend this entire month in Tokyo." Claudia said regretfully.

"Then I can come there if you want. I like Tokyo."

"Really?" Claudia asked, "That would be wonderful."

Three days later, after taking care of business in Frankfurt, Archer was flying to Tokyo.

After resting for a few hours, Archer got ready and reached Claudia's hotel.

"Hey you!" she welcomed him with open arms as they met. Archer could see Claudia looked good like her photographs online. "So how was work?" she asked.

After talking to her for a bit, Archer could see that this was a no nonsense woman who wore her heart on her sleeves. She was not pretending to be something else, and Archer had always liked independent women with a free spirit.

"How long have you been here?" Archer was surprised to see how much Claudia loved this city and its culture.

"Tokyo is my second home. I just love this city." Claudia had a big smile while talking about Tokyo. Archer could see that she was really in love with this city. "How much do you know about this city and its culture?" she asked Archer.

"Not much. I have been here only a few times." Archer said trying to impress Claudia. "Is Godzilla real?" He made a silly face after this silly question.

Claudia appreciated the joke and her laughter proved it to Archer, "Oh yes, he lives under the city. People here worship him and offer rich blonde American businessmen to him."

Archer liked this girl, but it was too good to be true. He could not believe that this girl was for real. She was rich and so did not care about Archer's money. She had a great sense of humor, and could joke about things she considered very dear. And she was not pretending to be something that she was not.

"What is her deal?" Archer thought to himself.

"What?" Claudia asked.

"Sorry?" Archer came out of his trance.

"I thought you said something." Claudia clarified.

"No, I am just really tired."

"I think I have the perfect solution for that." Claudia said with a mysterious smile.

"Is that some ancient Japanese herb that will make me feel rejuvenated?" Archer asked smiling. Claudia got up and fixed her hair.

"Better than that. Lets go, I will show you something."

Archer had no other plans and so both of them left the hotel.

They entered the cab and Claudia talked to the driver in Japanese.

"WOW!" Archer thought, "She is so awesome! There must be something very wrong with her."

Archer noticed Claudia was getting quite cosy with him in the cab. Not that he had a problem with it, but he was just surprised, that she was passing on subtle hints. She kept casually touching Archer on his hands and grabbed his shoulders while laughing.

Archer knew these signs and he could see that this woman was in a wild mood.

"Listen.." Claudia then revealed her intentions, "I hope you won't find it forthcoming, but I really really like you."

Archer did not know what to say but other than, "Well, I like you too."

A big seductive smile appeared on Claudia's lips, "Then I am going to give you a big surprise. Do you know where we are going?"

"I have no clue!" he replied.

"I am taking you to a very exotic place. Have you heard about the Love Hotels?" Claudia said staring into Archer's eyes.

"Love hotels? I guess I have read about them in some articles. These are hotels where people come to have sex. I guess."

"Yes!" Claudia whispered in Archer's ears very seductively, "These are found only in Japan and today we are going to my favorite Love Hotel."

"Favorite?" was the only word that stuck out in Archer's head. But his excitement took over his better judgment. Besides, Claudia was now frisking her hands all over his body.

"Am I ready for this?" he asked himself.

Suddenly the car stopped and the driver said something in Japanese. Claudia quickly paid him and opened the door. "We are here. Come!"

Claudia quickly got out, but Archer remained in the cab, thinking what he should do. "This is the first time I am meeting this woman and the first place she took me is a weird ass place where people come to fulfill their kinky sexual desires."

"Hey, come on!" Claudia cried from outside the cab.

Archer realized he had to do something and then he looked forward. He found the driver staring at him through the rear view mirror. Like a reflex, his hand moved and opened the door. His legs walked out of the car and he saw the cab driving away.

"Come!" Archer could see Claudia's inviting smile. Together, they entered this strange looking building.

The staff seemed familiar with Claudia as she walked inside. She kept talking to them in Japanese and the further they went, the more comfortable Archer got.

"Where is the restroom?" Archer asked Claudia.

She looked at him carefully, "Are you nervous, cowboy?"

Archer could see her silently laughing at him, "No, I wanted to pee since we left your hotel," he said with a straight face.

"Okay!" Claudia smiled and pointed him to a door. "There. Go and do your thing."

Archer quickly walked inside the restroom and locked the door. He opened the tap and pulled out his phone. He dialed Phillip's number and waited for the phone to ring.

"What?" Phillip's sleepy voice answered the phone.

"Dude, I think I bit more than I could chew this time." Archer was getting nervous.

"Tell me what is going on. You were absolutely fine when you were leaving to meet Claudia."

"This woman has brought me to her favorite Love Hotel. Do you know what a love hotel is?" Archer asked trying to keep his voice down.

"Yes I know what a love hotel is. You made me read those articles." Phillip said, "But if I remember correctly, you were quite intrigued with the concept of such hotels. What happened now?"

"Did you not hear me? It's her _favorite_ love hotel in Tokyo. Favorite is the key word, in case you missed it again." Archer almost screamed, but he covered his face with the other hand.

"So, just go ahead and have fun." Phillip chuckled.

"This is so not funny, Man!" Archer replied.

"Hey, all you need to do is get to the airport and come back. You are not in 1942. Nobody there can hold you against your will."

Archer could see that Phillip was right. Nothing was holding him there and he did not want to experience this weird Japanese obsession of a place where people come to have random unconventional sex.

"Alright! I am coming home." Archer said gaining his confidence back.

Hours later, he was back at the airport, waiting for his flight. He was trying to forget Claudia's disgusted face when he told her that he did not want to do this. Lucky for him, she did not create a scene or behave like a crazy chick. To his surprise, she took it very maturely. "I understand, this is not for everyone. It needs a certain taste and courage," she said being a little dismissive of Archer.

But the only thing Archer cared about was getting the hell out of there.

"Fuck this shit!" he took out his phone and deleted his profile from the High Seas website. Then he uninstalled the app from his phone as well. "What kind of moron came up with this idea!" He was relieved he was going home, safe and sound.

Chapter 3

"You look stunning! Good luck with the date," Jane typed in her phone below the picture of Vera in her blue dress.

Vera received a confidence boost on reading Jane's comment and she looked at herself in the mirror again. This was the Vera she was missing for a long time. She was going on a date with a handsome man she had met at work.

"Are you ready?" Alice asked from downstairs.

"Yes Mom!" Vera replied admiring herself. She quickly checked her purse and exited her room. Her mother was waiting for her downstairs.

"Wow! You look so beautiful! This dress looks so lovely on you." Alice had nothing but praises for her daughter.

"Thanks Mom. Are you sure you will be fine by yourself?" Vera asked.

"I am not a little child Vera. You go and have fun."

"Promise me, you will call me if you need anything." Vera held her mother's hand tightly.

"I promise, I will call you. Now go." Alice said.

Vera kissed her mother and left the house. She got into a taxi and reached the restaurant where she was supposed to meet her date.

Cyril was a charming young man who was clearly impressed by Vera's beauty. Vera could see that he was out of words when he first saw her in person. "Wow!" was the only word that came out of his mouth.

"Still got it!" Vera high five-d herself in her imagination. "You look great, Cyril!" she knew she should pay him a compliment as well. The guy blushed and took her inside the restaurant.

Cyril could see Vera was a little shy and so he decided to break the ice. "How is life Vera?" he threw a very vague question at her.

"Good!" Vera replied and went back to being shy.

Cyril could sense that this would be a little tougher than he thought, and so he tried again, "You like this place? Its one of my favorite restaurants in the city."

Vera looked around and did not find anything that she did not like, "I like it."

Cyril now knew for sure that there was something strange here. "Tell me Vera, do you go out often?"

Vera was stumped. She did not know how to answer that. Should she say 'No' and come out as a dork who lives in her closet, or say 'Hell Yeah!' and risk being tagged as a slut? There was no gray area for her. She thought her answer would be either black or plain white.

Cyril could see her confusion, but did not understand the reason behind it. However, he waited patiently for Vera to come up with an answer.

"I used to go out a lot, you know, when I was in college." Vera had already started explaining herself. "But now I mostly stay at home."

Cyril nodded trying to seem polite, but he could sense how awkward Vera was being. He really liked this girl and so he was willing to give her as many chances she wanted to have this evening.

"Well, I come out here a lot with my friends. You and your friends don't go out much?" he asked trying to make Vera talk.

"Not really! We just stay home and talk. Mostly we watch movies on the internet."

Cyril jumped on the first opening he saw, "Hey I love watching movies too. What kind of movies do you like?"

Suddenly, Vera realized that she knew the answer to this question. "Documentaries mostly. I like learning about new things. But my friend Jane likes romance and dramas. I guess a stereotypical female movie buff."

Cyril saw Vera's beautiful smile for the first time that evening and he wanted to see more of it. He kept talking to her about movies and things she liked. Vera surprised herself by opening to this charming man about her likes and dislikes. She told him about her secret love for adventure sports. "I used to trek and go kayaking when I was in college. And I really wish to do that again."

After their wonderful dinner, Cyril turned to Vera and looked into her eyes, "Vera, I really enjoyed this evening with you."

Vera was astonished. She was not expecting this on her first date, but she decided to go with the flow. "Me too!" she said bringing a smile to her beautiful face.

"Would you like me to drop you home?" Cyril asked like a gentleman and Vera nodded in agreement with a smile.

The ride to Vera's home was fun like their dinner. They discussed so many things and Vera laughed out loud a few times. The car stopped and Cyril looked at Vera. Their eyes met and Vera found herself moving towards Cyril.

Cyril took the hint and closed the distance between their faces. Their lips met and electricity filled Vera's body. She had not been touched by a guy in years and suddenly she remembered how great it felt. In an instance, she grabbed Cyril's face and pulled him towards herself. Both of them passionately made out in his car. But then, Vera saw her house across the road, and she closed her eyes.

Cyril noticed something was not right, "What happened?" he asked.

Vera opened her eyes and decided that tonight, she will get out of her shell. She wanted to be the old Vera who did not shy away from getting what she wanted.

"Can we go to your place?" she asked.

Cyril did not know how to answer that question. He waited for a moment to make sure that he was not dreaming, "Of course! But are you sure?" he confirmed.

Vera grabbed his face and kissed him again, "Yes!" she said.

Cyril quickly put on the seat belt and drove away.

*****

Cyril and Vera were lying in Cyril's bed without their clothes. They were feeling the warmth of each other's bodies and their hands were exploring the spaces their hearts desired. They took a brief moment to just pause and look into each other's eyes. Vera could not believe that it was happening. Her eyes gave Cyril the permission he needed.

He prepared himself and just when he was ready, the bed vibrated. It was Vera's phone.

"I am so sorry!" she said almost pushing Cyril away. It was her mother who was calling her. "Uggh! I am sure it can wait." Vera's excitement took over and she silenced the ringer.

"I am sorry, where were we?" she asked with a cute smile. Cyril got ready again, but soon after that the phone vibrated again. Vera checked and it was her mother calling again.

"Hey Mom!" Vera looked into Cyril's eyes who was towering over her. She signaled him to wait for a minute with her finger. Cyril knew this could take a bit longer than that and he laid down beside Vera.

"Where are you? You said you will be back by 10." Alice said.

"Mom, I am running a little late. Do not wait for me and go to sleep. I will be home late tonight.." she looked at Cyril who was smiling at her, ".. or probably in the morning."

"There is another reason why I called you." her mother said.

"What?" Vera was now a little alarmed, "Are you okay Mom?" she got up in the bed.

"The cable is out. I am not able to watch TV." Alice complained.

"What?" Vera did not expect this from her mother, "What do you want me to do?"

"You fix it all the time for me. I don't know how to take care of it." Alice explained.

"So you want me to leave my date and come home to fix your cable?" Vera made sure her mother heard how ridiculous it sounded.

"You told me to call you if I needed anything." Alice said.

"I meant in an emergency. Like if you were feeling unwell. Or if somebody was in the house." Vera almost yelled at her, but remembering that she was with Cyril, she controlled herself.

"I am sorry, I did not know that I was only supposed to disturb you when my life was in danger." Alice tried to sound sarcastic.

Cyril got out of the bed and went to the bathroom. Vera saw him locking the door.

"Mom, I am really in no position to talk about this right now," she said clenching her teeth.

"You know I can't sleep without watching a movie on the classics channel." Alice reminded Vera as if the TV was a cure for her ailment.

Cyril came out of the bathroom wearing a t-shirt. "Holy shit!" Vera said to herself. This guy had abandoned the hopes of having sex. He was dressed.

"Mom, I am sorry but if you want to watch your movie, you will have to take a shot at fixing it yourself tonight. I will be back in the morning. Alright? Goodnight!" Vera hung up before Alice was even able to say anything. She than looked at Cyril who was lying by her in the bed.

"You are wearing a shirt?" she asked hinting at the obvious.

"I thought you guys would take long and I was feeling cold." Cyril explained.

"Well, I am available now." Vera smiled.

Cyril looked into her eyes and believed her. He slowly took off his shirt and leaned in to kiss her. As they kissed, their hands surfed over each other's bodies and Cyril gently placed Vera under his body.

"You ready now?" he asked jokingly, to which Vera chuckled and nodded in agreement.

Readying himself, Cyril was about to enter Vera when the bed vibrated again.

"Fuck!" Vera cried checking her phone — it was her mother again.

"Mom, it better be some emergency now." she yelled ignoring Cyril.

What Alice told her over the phone, made Vera wear her clothes quickly.

"I am so sorry for this Cyril, but this is an emergency."

"I understand." the guy said.

Vera reached the door and then turned around, "Would you mind dropping me home? I don't know if I will get a cab at this hour."

Cyril stared at Vera's face with an open mouth.

*****

"I am so sorry. Lets do it again some other time." Vera said as Cyril dropped her home.

"Yeah sure!" Cyril said and drove off without waiting for Vera to respond or even smile. She knew her date was ruined and so she turned towards her home that was covered with darkness.

"MOM!" she yelled while entering the dark house.

"Here!" Alice called for her from a corner. Vera reached the source of the sound and found her mother with a flashlight, trying to figure out the electrical circuit board of the house.

"Who asked you to play with this at this time of the night, Mom? Do you even know how this works?" Vera knew that her mother knew nothing about fixing the electricity.

"You did! You asked me to fix it myself." Alice came back.

Vera took off her sandals and wore slippers, "I asked you to fix the cable, not push yourself into the dark ages."

Alice threw the flashlight on the ground and stormed off in anger, "You know what? Go to hell! I am trying to be nice and you are being a brat!"

"Don't walk into a wall!" Vera screamed seeing her mother walking into the dark. She then picked up the flashlight and looked at the circuit board. Two of the fuses were fried and needed to be replaced. Vera walked to the store room and started looking for the spare fuses. After picking them up, she opened the door and found an old face staring at her, "Whoa!" Vera jumped back dropping the fuses on the floor.

"What?" Alice wondered.

"Mom! You gave me a mini heart attack!" Vera held her chest breathing heavily.

"Don't talk like that. You know I don't like that kind of talk." Alice said in a stern voice.

Vera realized her mistake. Her father died of a sudden heart attack and so her mother did not like it to be mentioned even as a figure of speech. Heart problems were taboo in the Jones's house.

"I am sorry! You know I didn't mean that." Vera said looking at her mother.

"I am sorry too." Alice said in an apologetic tone, "I ruined your date, didn't I?"

Alice saw no point in dragging this futile feud any further. She took a step closer to her mom and hugged her tightly. "It's okay Mom. I will find another one."

"Was he good?" Alice asked hugging her daughter.

"Oh yeah. He was a peach." Vera smiled.

They finally broke their hug and Alice complained, "You never take me seriously."

"Alright, yes, he was really nice Mom!" Vera said in a simple tone. "Happy?"

Alice nodded with a smile.

"Okay, let me fix the electricity now." Vera picked up the fuses from the floor but one of them was broken.

"Oh lord!" Alice exclaimed.

"Don't worry, I am sure there are more in the store room." Vera checked the shelf but there were no more spare fuses left.

"Looks like we are going to spend this night in the dark ages" Vera said while walking out of the store room with her mother.

"You mind sleeping with me tonight?" Alice asked.

Vera could not say no, "Of course Mom." She kissed her hand.

*****

It was a Sunday and Vera came back home in the morning with spare fuses and some other supplies. She fixed the electricity and went back to her room. The first thing she checked was her email and social media, but there was no response from Cyril. She had been constantly checking her phone every minute since last night, but Cyril did not messaged her even once.

Wanting to call him, she stopped herself. "This looks so desperate," she said, knowing that she was indeed desperate. She really liked Cyril and needed one more chance to prove that being with her was not a bad idea. But she could not blame the guy, for what happened last night was a disaster for a first date.

And so she called the only person she could talk to about this.

"You did what?" Jane asked. "Are you out of your mind? You asked him to take you home on your first date? What do you think he would think of you?"

Vera knew Jane was right, but it felt right in that moment. Besides, it was all fine till her mother called and ruined everything.

"I don't know. Things were feeling so right for the first time in years. And I decided to not care anymore." Vera tried to justify her actions.

"You don't jump in the sack with someone on your first date. How hard is that to remember?" Jane's voice came out screeching through the phone.

"Hey, it was all good till Mom called." Vera yelled back.

"Maybe it was a sign from God, telling you to get the fuck out of there." Jane did not lower her voice. And now Vera was feeling like an idiot.

"I know I fucked up. But what can I do now?" she asked.

"Nothing. And whatever you do, don't call him." Jane told her.

"But I really liked him." Vera said in a desperate tone.

"Let him go babe. Let him go. There are plenty of fish in the sea." Jane said like a philosopher.

"But what if the same thing happens when I am with a different fish?" Vera wondered, "I need complete piece of mind when I am on a date."

"What are you talking about?" Jane asked.

"I am telling you, it was all good till I received that first call from Mom." Vera paused for a moment to choose her words carefully. "I don't think I will be able to focus on any relationship because I need to focus more on my Mom."

Jane did not say a word.

"Don't get me wrong, I love my Mom and there is no way I am going to leave her, but there is no way for me to have a normal relationship until she is taken care of."

"So any guy who wants to be with you, has to take your Mom with you?" Jane simplified Vera's problem in a small sentence, "Like one of those package deals. Right?"

This made Vera chuckle, "Yeah, I guess. My mom comes with me. We are a package deal. And until somebody wants this deal, I am not leaving the shelf."

Vera and Jane shared a good laugh discussing this scenarios, unaware that Alice was listening to them from the hallway.

*****

It was another hectic day at the airport. The flights were grounded again, but not because of the bad weather. Weather was in fact beautiful. The reason was the raised level of terror threat. The whole airport was going crazy. Passengers were asked to stay in the main lounge and nobody was allowed to leave the building. Air Marshals were closely observing the crowd for any potential threat, while the TSA staff was being smug as ever.

"Fuck these people!" Vera heard a passenger yelling in frustration. This was the second time in the month when they were facing a horde of irate passengers. The biggest issue was that they themselves had no idea what was going on. Nobody was updating them on any issue and Vera and her colleagues were left to their own devices.

"I am sorry Sir, but we will inform you as soon as we get an update on the situation. We apologize for this inconvenience." This was the verbatim they were ordered to say to every passenger. And the fact that nobody was supposed to get their refund did not help at all. The airlines were clear on their policy; it was not their fault that the flights were grounded or delayed. They were ready to fly away and so no passenger was entitled to get a refund. Besides, nobody was allowed to leave the building and so there was no chance of changing the mode of transport.

"This is insane!" Vera said to Jane while handling the long line of passengers. "They are not even telling us what is going on."

"You know what? Just follow my lead." Jane said winking at her. Vera curiously looked at how she handled her next passenger.

"Hello Sir, We are so sorry for this inconvenience but I hope you understand how important your security is for us and the concerned authorities."

The passenger tried to understand what Jane meant, and Jane kept going on. She pretended to check on her computer, "Well, we are ready to fly you off as soon as we get a go ahead from the airport security. As you can see.." she subtly diverted the passenger's gaze towards the armed unit that was standing behind the line, "we are leaving no stone unturned." By now the passenger was starting to feel as if he was playing a part in a big patriotic scheme, "And we will inform you as soon as we are ready to take off. Meanwhile, please accept our gratitude for keeping America safe."

Vera could see that nothing Jane said made any sense, but the passenger was eating it from her hands. She saw two more passengers being sold that same bullshit and so she decided it was time for her to do the same thing, "Hello Sir, We are sorry for this inconvenience, but I hope you understand how important your security is for us."

The passenger nodded in agreement and Vera could see a sense of gratitude on her face.

"Damn Jane is good!" she said to herself.

Both of them took care of the long line and only a few passengers snapped out at them. For them, it was better than most of their Mondays. After taking care of the whole line, they decided to treat themselves.

Showing their airline ID cards, they gained access to the VIP lounge and sat down with their coffee and cakes.

"Now you understand how smooth I am?" Jane patted her own back.

"Yes, I do." Vera admired her friend.

"This is total crap!" both of them heard a voice from their side. Two men were sitting together at a table adjacent to them.

*****

Archer was about to fly off his handle. He slammed the magazine he was reading on the table in an attempt to get Phillip's attention — "Are you even listening to me?" he said, to which, Phillip slowly raised his gaze and looked into Archer's eyes.

"Yes, I am listening. But what can we do about it? It's an issue of national security. You know how paranoid they get with things like that." Phillip explained nonchalantly.

"I understand that terrorists might try to board a regular commercial flight. But why are they grounding the private fliers? There is no terrorist in my jet." Archer was on a rant.

"You know they can't let any airplane fly until the threat level goes down. Why are you talking like this?" Phillip looked at Archer and waited for him to answer.

"What do you mean? I always talk like this." Archer said.

"No! There is something strange with you since you came back from Tokyo."

Archer could see a smirk on Phillip's face.

"Screw you! I dodged a bullet there and you are making fun of me?"

Phillip just smiled and shrugged.

"She was a crazy woman and I am glad I got off easy. God knows what she was planning to do to me."

Jane and Vera could not help from chuckling on hearing this. Phillip and Archer gave them 'the look' that made the girls turn their faces away in embarrassment of getting caught.

"I want to get out of here!" Archer demanded. "Call somebody and get my jet off the ground."

Phillip did as he was asked. He checked his contact list and made a call. "Hey Eric, there is a little problem. We need to get our jet in the air and their is a lock down at this airport."

Jane and Vera were constantly listening to the conversation at the table adjacent to them.

"He really thinks he can bypass the security and fly off when everybody else is grounded?" astonished, Vera asked Jane.

"Alright! Thanks." Phillip hung up and looked at Archer, "Eric said, he will get it sorted in around. We should be in air in 10 minutes."

"Unbelievable!" Jane scoffed listening to Phillip. It again drew the attention of Phillip and Archer to them.

"Excuse me?" Phillip turned to Jane. "Is there a problem?"

"Why did you think so?" Jane replied in the same tone.

Phillip decided it was best to not say anything else.

"Lets just get out of here." Archer suggested to his friend and both of the them left the lounge. Jane saw them walk out while Vera chuckled silently.

"What assholes! They are actually going to bypass the whole security? Are we not humans?" Jane said.

"Ooh! I have a private jet and I want to fly away from these filthy poor people." Vera tried to mock Archer and Phillip.

"Daddy, I am stuck at this airport with these poor people. Please get me out of here." Jane joined in.

"I swear to God, I am never going to date anybody like that." Vera declared.

"He owned a private jet. How would you come across a billion-aire to reject him as your date?" Jane asked.

"Hey, I was talking about his personality. Such a douchebag." Vera clarified.

"Major douchebag!" Jane added and Vera nodded.

*****

Archer was looking out of the window of his jet. He could see all the planes on the airstrip and the sky was clear. His was the only plane that was in the air.

"Why do you think those girls were laughing at us?"

"Are you serious?" Phillip said, "You know why. Cause you are rich and powerful. You took off from that airport when everyone else is still stuck there."

"That's just the surface. Go deeper!" Archer smiled at Phillip.

Phillip did not want to play this game anymore, "I am not a psychiatrist. Just tell me what you think."

Archer looked out of the window one more time and then looked back at Phillip. "That was their defense mechanism kicking in."

Archer saw Phillip looking at him with a blank face.

"All of us, are afraid of something or the other." Archer explained. "For instance, I am afraid that people are going to use me for their personal gains. That is why I freaked out in Tokyo, because I realized I was just an sex object for Claudia."

"Where are you going with this?" Phillip asked looking confused.

"Just hear me out." Archer assured him that he was on the right track, "So when I figured out Claudia's real intentions, I freaked out. That — was my defense mechanism. Whenever I panic, I freak out and try to run away."

"Okay!" Phillip continued staring at Archer.

"So some people deal with their fears by running away, while some deal with it by laughing at it. It's not a genuine laugh, but a petty one."

"So you are telling me that those girls at the airport were laughing at us because they were afraid of us?" Phillip asked.

"Not afraid of us." Archer clarified. "But intimidated. I have seen this many times. Especially in boarding school. Some kids used to laugh at me only because my family was deemed better than theirs."

"Where did you learn this shrink stuff? Boarding school?" Phillip wondered.

"Documentaries!" Archer replied. "You should invest some time in them too. Instead of watching those girly dramas you like."

"Hey, we discussed respecting each other's choices. Remember?" Phillip said angrily.

"Alright! Jeez!" Archer chuckled.

Phillip went back to reading his magazine while Archer looked out of the window again. There was something in that laughter that did not make him mad or angry. For the first time in years after his boarding school, somebody had disliked him for his money. Though he did not tell Phillip about it, he felt really good, knowing that his money had no value to a person sitting next to him. Those girls knew Archer was very rich, but still they did not care for his money.

He kept thinking about it during the whole trip.

*****

Sitting in his rec room, Archer opened his laptop and googled dating sites. One specific result stood out to him — It was a website for adventure lovers. Archer instantly clicked on it and looked around. He liked how the site felt and decided to make a profile for himself. He added all the details except how much he earned or what he did. And so when it came to put in his profession, Archer thought long and hard about what to write in there. The only thing he could remember was the girls laughing at him at the airport.

"Hmmm!" he suddenly had an idea and started typing — 'Aviation Industry.'

To him, it was not a lie, because he owned two Jets and so it counted as being in the industry. After all he was paying for the maintenance of his two jets. Besides, he had a degree in aeronautical engineering.

"Perfect!" Archer smiled seeing his completed profile.

*****

"Are you sure?" Vera asked Jane who was on the other end of the phone.

"Hell yeah! I got to know about this website from a friend. You are going to love this." Jane was all praises for this website and so Vera opened it.

It was the same dating site for adventure lovers.

"I know how much you like these things. Maybe you will find somebody really nice here." Jane said.

Vera thought before doing anything and she took the website in through her eyes.

"Alright!" she said and started creating her profile, "Done!" she said after finishing it.

"That's my girl!" Jane cried in admiration, "Now go and browse some handsome dudes."

Vera heeded Jane's advice and started browsing the website.

Chapter 4

After a busy week, Archer got some time to unwind. He decided to spend the whole week going on a trek in South America.

"When will you be back?" Phillip asked him.

"After a week. You will handle things here by yourself," Archer joked.

"I didn't want to tell you, but I have been planning to usurp your business. Soon it will be all mine and you are going to work for me." Phillip replied with a straight face.

"That's it? I thought you had more evil inside you than that."

"Unlike you, some of us have to work here. So call me if you need anything." Phillip replied.

"Okay buddy. You do the same."

"Sure thing Archie! Take care." Phillip replied and got busy with his work.

Archer left the country and started his trek. He found a guide who introduced him to some of the most amazing routes through few small villages in Chile. He enjoyed every bit of it, but to his surprise the trek ended after only four days. And on the 6th day, Archer was back in his rec room.

"Where are you? I have an extra day to not work." Archer called Phillip.

"I am busy here. I am sure you can come up with something for a day. Be creative." Phillip told him. He was unavailable and so Archer had to find something to do by himself.

Suddenly, he remembered about this website he stumbled upon weeks ago. He opened his laptop and logged into his account. The website had a few matches for him. And then, Archer's eyes grew wide. He instantly recognized Vera's picture from the airport. The girl who ridiculed him for being rich.

He chuckled for a bit and then clicked on Vera's profile. Turned out that the website had suggested her to Archer because they both were in the aviation industry and also because Vera was interested in trekking.

"Wow!" Archer was really impressed by her pictures. Though they seemed really old, Vera's pictures gained her Archer's admiration. Intrigued, he read her profile word to word and felt an urge to know her. Her profile had her twitter and instagram linked in and so Archer decided to take a virtual stroll and know more about Vera.

Whatever he found about this beautiful girl impressed him. And after a few minutes and several megabytes of looking around Vera's social media accounts, Archer could not resist himself from sending a friend request on the website. Now he waited for her to reply back.

*****

Vera was at work when she received a notification on her phone. It was from the dating site she had joined last night. At first, she could not determine what this was all about.

"What is this?" she said unlocking her phone with confusion. In her emails, there was a notification of her receiving a friend request.

Jane looked at it and she instantly identified it. "It's from that dating site silly. Looks like you have a new friend request."

Vera clicked the link in the email and she was quickly taken to her profile. "Archer.." she read the name.

"Archer what??" Jane inquired.

"Don't know. There is just Archer, no last name." Vera read again making sure she did not miss anything. Jane quickly took the phone from her hands, "Show it to me."

Jane's eyes grew wide as she browsed Archer's profile. "Ooh, he is handsome! Look at that hair."

Vera looked at Archer's pictures and he indeed had beautiful hair.

"I just hope that is not a wig." Jane joked and then gave the phone back to Vera. "So, what are you waiting for? Accept his request."

"What?" Vera said. "He is a complete stranger."

"Maybe you are forgetting how online dating works, you meet a random stranger and then get to know them. That is precisely the reason why the internet was created." Jane finished.

"You need to read more about the internet. I am pretty sure that is not the reason behind the creation of the internet." Vera put the phone back in her pocket.

"What are you doing? Accept that handsome man's friend request." Jane ordered.

"In case you have forgotten, we are at work. I don't know about you, but I need to focus on what I am supposed to do here." Vera sarcastically reminded Jane where they were.

"Jeez!" Jane scoffed at Vera's attitude. "I hope you don't talk like that on your dates."

Vera gave Jane a piercing stare that she returned with an equally strong gaze. Both of them chuckled at their childish competition and went back to work.

"But seriously, you need to meet that blonde dude. He looks hot as fuck!" Jane said getting back to her work.

"I will check it out at home." Vera said trying to get Archer's handsome face out of her mind. She was trying really hard, but Archer was not leaving her head.

*****

Back at home, Vera sat down in her bed after dinner. Her phone buzzed and she picked it up. It was a message from Jane — "Accept the blondie."

Vera chuckled at Jane's eagerness and put the phone under her pillow. She then picked up her laptop and opened it. After logging onto that site, she was now looking at Archer's friend request. The cursor moved and clicked on Archer's name. Vera was now looking at his profile. His smile was looking more intoxicating on a bigger screen. And in this moment, Vera realized that Jane was right about his hair — they were magnificent.

She browsed through a few pictures in his profile that showed him on various treks and expeditions. "Is that North Pole?" Vera wondered looking at a photo. Archer was completely covered with heavy jackets, masks, safety goggles and snow boots. He was in knee deep snow.

Vera looked at that picture for around a minute. She had always wanted to go to a place like that, a place that was untouched by humans. But with her job and mother, she never had a chance to even plan things out for her. But Archer's pictures reminded her of all the places she wanted to visit and the things she wanted to do. This was the life she wanted to live, and this stranger was living it. For a moment, Vera felt envious of Archer, but then she realized how stupid it was.

The cursor moved and she clicked on 'Accept'. Archer was the first entry in her friend list.

*****

Archer got a notification on his phone while he was in a meeting. Phillip saw the smile on his friend's face. He knew this smile had nothing to do with the boring meeting they were in. But suddenly, Archer was a changed man — the man who seemed bored to death was now smiling ear to ear. Everybody in that room was able to see this change. Archer put the phone back into his pocket and focused on the job at hand.

"What was that?" Phillip asked as they both got in the car.

"What?" Archer had no clue what Phillip was talking about, but his smile was still there on his face.

Phillip reminded him of the sudden change in his spirit and Archer's smile widened.

"You remember the girls from the airport?" he looked at Phillip.

"The ones who hated how rich you were?" Phillip's memory needed no jogging. He remembered that day.

"Yup! I just became friends with one of them." Archer replied.

"Okay..." Phillip responded, taking a deep breath. "And why is it making you all smiley?"

"After decades, somebody hated me because I have money. It feels good." Archer told Phillip the secret behind his happiness.

"You are weird. You know that, right?" Phillip looked Archer straight in his eyes. But Archer kept smiling.

*****

Vera was in her bed, when her phone buzzed again. Jane had been pestering her to know if Archer had initiated any kind of communication.

"I swear to God, I will block this woman." Vera said, taking out her phone from under the pillow. But to her surprise it was not Jane. It was another notification email from the website. Archer had sent her a message.

Quickly, Vera picked up her laptop and signed into her account. Within seconds she was now in her inbox. She started reading Archer's message, "Hey there, fellow trekker here. I saw your pictures, and was thoroughly impressed."

A smile danced on Vera's face that was illuminated by the laptop's bright screen. She kept staring at the message for sometime and then started typing —

"Thanks! I loved your pictures too. Especially the one where you are knee deep in the snow. Was that from an expedition? I have always wanted to go to such a place."

Vera's fingers furiously danced on the keys when she suddenly realized that she might be revealing too much for her first interaction. She saw Archer's message and realized how brief and to the point it was. She decided to write something short and witty. Something that would prove that she is a sensible person. And so she sat in front of her laptop, thinking what to write.

Then, it hit her — she pulled the laptop closer to her and started typing again.

"Thanks! Saw your pictures too. Really enjoyed them. Hope to see more."

She read it again and again to make sure that there was no error in her words and spellings. The one thing she did not want was to come out as a poser who did not know how to write a proper sentence. After being satisfied with her sentence, she then pressed 'Send' and stared at the screen with anticipation. The tiny clock at the bottom of her message rotated and then a tiny 'Sent' appeared in its place. Her message was delivered.

"Ding!" a sweet sound played on the laptop. Archer had replied to her message.

"Well I guess we are mutual admirers. I enjoyed your pictures too. Where was the one taken where you are on a bike? I loved that place."

Vera was not feeling much nervous anymore. She started typing again, "That picture is 5 years old. It's a trail in Jefferson City. One of my favorites. Sorry, but I have not trekked or hiked for years now."

Vera waited for Archer's response and it came in just one word, "Why?"

"My job I guess. But I so want to start again." Vera typed and hit send.

Archer replied, "I would be honored to accompany you on your next adventure."

Vera just gaped at this reply. She was thinking when this handsome man was about to ask her out and she did not have to wait for long. But she had no clue how to respond to this message. She wanted to type, "YES YES YES YES!" in all caps and underlined, but she knew better.

"I hope I did not alarm you with my forwardness.." another message from Archer popped on the screen.

Vera knew how to respond to that, "Nothing like that. And I would be glad to have an experienced partner on my next adventure."

"So where do you want to go? I know this great trail in Chile. I was there a few weeks ago." Archer typed.

Vera laughed at the last reply. She was not planning to go that far, "I was thinking for a little local adventure." She typed with a smile on her face.

"Ohh.. sorry!" popped on the screen with a silly face emoticon.

"There is an adventure club in our city. Want to tag along this weekend? We can climb some artificial walls." Vera responded.

"Absolutely!" Archer's response was short and precise.

"Great! I will share the location of the place with you. We can meet there around noon."

"Will be there." Archer responded.

Vera thought that it was best to end this conversation right here. She did not want to ruin a good moment by talking too much.

"Alrighty then, see you there on Saturday." she typed.

Archer got the hint and replied with "Sure!" and a smiley face. The conversation stopped right there.

Vera smiled while looking at Archer's picture.

*****

It was a Saturday afternoon. The traffic was a breeze and Vera was standing outside the club. She looked at the big sign-board one more time, 'The Rush' it said in big red and green block letters over the building. Vera had a her bag of gym clothes and accessories with her. She checked the time and it was 12:27. Her eyes were looking for a blonde man walking towards her. "I should have given him my number," she thought.

After waiting for Archer outside she decided to wait inside the club. After paying for just one session, she reached the wall climb area. The club did not have too many people and Vera liked it that way. She had been here a few times earlier. This was the only thread that connected her to her passion of adventure. She placed her bag on a bench and started warming up.

"Vera Jones?" Archer's deep voice was picked up by Vera's ears. As she turned around she found Archer standing in front of her.

"WOW!" her brain screamed inside her head. Archer's pictures did no justice to how handsome he looked in real life. But this guy was lost in the beautiful eyes of this star-struck lady.

"Archer?" Vera asked with wide eyes.

"Yes, it's me." He extended his hand to her. "It's so nice to meet you."

"When did you come?" Vera asked shaking his hand, "I waited for you outside the club."

"Then I guess we both were waiting for each other. I arrived here well before noon." Archer replied. Vera was relieved that this guy was not making her wait. In fact he was here early.

"So, how do you want to start?" Archer asked looking at one wall that was free. "Ladies first?" he looked at Vera with a charming smile.

Vera obliged and stepped forward. Both of them got ready.

"You want to use the safety lines?" Archer asked Vera.

"Please! I am not a kid." Vera said with a smug smile.

"Oh yeah?" Archer said to herself. This girl was ready to compete with him. "Alright, go ahead. Show me what you can do."

Vera took her position at the bottom of the wall and before pressing the timer, she turned back and looked at Archer, "Remember, I am doing it after weeks."

Archer just smiled at her as Vera got ready. Her hands pressed the timer and she moved like lightning on that wall. Grabbing and stepping over one support after another, she did not seem out of practice.

Archer was enjoying it like a dance performance. Vera's technique was flawless. Soon, she was at the top and like a reflex, her hand pressed the timer that was there. With the same speed and flow, she was back to the ground within seconds. Vera stopped the timer and looked at her time — 31.2 Seconds.

"Not bad!" Archer admired. "I saw you were using the static climb. Quite impressive for a beginner."

Vera scoffed with laughter, "Oh yeah? Let me see how you do."

Archer winked at her from the bottom of the wall and pressed the timer. In one sweeping motion, Archer jumped from one support to another and pulled himself up. Repeating this jumping and pulling he was at the top within seconds. From there he looked at Vera and smiled. She was certainly impressed.

As Archer came back and stopped the timer, his time read — 29 Seconds.

Vera clapped for her friend as he approached her.

"You like what you saw?" he asked with a naughty smile.

"Oh yeah! I have always admired people who use the Dead Point technique." Vera admitted.

"Well, I learned from the best. I met a Sherpa in India who taught me climbing." Archer said relaxing his hands.

"India?" Vera wondered, "Where else have you been in the world? What do you do?"

Archer realized that his mouth had landed him in trouble, "I work in.. Aviation!" he thought quickly on his feet. "And so I keep flying around the world."

Vera grew envious of this man, "Lucky you! I have always wanted such a job."

Archer wanted to offer her to come with him, but he decided to keep his mouth shut. He just looked at her and smiled.

"So, another round? I am going to beat you this time." Vera challenged Archer.

"Lets do it!" Archer was game.

The two climbed several times, trying to best each other. Vera did beat Archer's time in a few tries, but Archer kept improving. At the end both of them were not able to decide who was the better climber.

"I guess we both have so much to learn from each other." Archer was being humble.

"I agree!" Vera wiped her sweat.

Vera was feeling so happy. This man was not only supporting her but also motivating her to do better. This is exactly the kind of man she had been looking for, and now he was standing right in front of her. She wanted to say a lot of things and tell him all her secrets and desires. And then, her bag vibrated and a loud ring smashed her chain of thoughts.

"Sorry!" she said and opened her bag to check her phone. It was her mother.

Vera suddenly remembered why she was shying away from a good relationship all these years. "Hello Mom!" she answered the call with a smile, "Everything okay?"

"Everything is fine. I just called to ask how is your date going?" Alice said.

"It's not a date Mom!" Vera covered her mouth and lowered her voice. "I am just wall climbing with a friend."

"Oh I know what that is. Don't try to lie to me." Alice knew what was really up.

"Mom, I will talk to you later."

"Just have fun, sweetheart!" Alice reminded her.

Vera put her phone back in the bag and looked at Archer, "Sorry that was my mother. You know how they are."

Archer just stared at her and then nodded in a 'No' — "I am afraid I don't know. My mother passed away when I was little."

Vera had no idea what to say next and so she just stared at him. Archer could see her face going red with awkwardness.

"You want to eat something? I am feeling a little hungry." he said, changing the tone and topic of their conversation.

Vera jumped at this opportunity, "Definitely! Lets get out of here."

They both left the club after changing into their normal clothes.

*****

Outside, both of them grabbed hot dogs and kept walking. The two of them were exchanging notes on their techniques. While talking to Vera, Archer realized that he had not explored the trails of his own country. All his life he had been traveling across the world looking for adventure. And in this mad rush, he overlooked all the great treks and trails in his country.

"I really want to go to that trail in Jefferson City." Archer confessed while taking a bite off his hot dog.

Vera remembered how beautiful it was years ago when she was there. "I don't know how that place is now. I just hope people have not killed it. You know how young people are."

Archer stopped for a brief moment and looked at Vera's face. He smiled and said, "You say that like you are old. I am sure you are also *young people*. Don't sell yourself short."

Archer walked ahead after finishing his sentence, but Vera was left fixed in her spot. In recent years, she had accepted that she did not look young, but this man could see that spark inside her.

"What are you waiting for? Come on." Archer called her out. Vera quickly came out of her day dreaming and walked to-wards Archer. But something crashed into her, making her hot dog meet with her top.

"Fuck!" the short man who bumped into Vera cried.

Archer ran to pick Vera up, "Are you okay?" he said looking at her.

"Watch where you're walking, Missy!" the man lectured Vera adjusting his bag.

"Practice what your preach Mister!" Archer delivered a stern reply to him. The man looked at Archer's face and remained fix with awe. Archer read his face and quickly got out of there taking Vera with him.

The man stood there, looking at Archer and Vera until they disappeared in the crowd. He then quickly took out his cellphone and dialed a number.

"Hello! Is this Finch Enterprises?" he asked. "My name is Victor Cooper, and I am a photojournalist. Could you connect me to Archer Finch, please?"

He tried to find Archer in the crowd, but saw only horde of random strangers, "Oh he is not in the country right now? No problem, I get it. Thanks."

Victor put his phone back in his pocket, "I think I know where Archer Finch is, but who was that lady with him?"

Victor entered a coffee shop and secured a table for himself. He opened his bag and along with two cameras and several lenses, a laptop was neatly stuffed in there. He pulled out his laptop and opened the web browser.

"Popular African American Models." He typed into the search browser. In the image section, he kept browsing through all the images, but no face matched the woman he saw with Archer Finch.

Tired, he then searched for Archer Finch and to his disappointment, not many images surfaced. The only images of Archer were of his young age when he took over his family business. Archer was known to keep a low profile and despite being a billionaire there were not many pictures of him available on the internet. Though by looking at the available resources, Victor was certain that it was Archer whom he saw earlier. But he was more interested in that lady with him.

Though he introduced himself as a Photo journalist, Victor Cooper was actually a paparazzi photographer. Stalking mid level celebrities was his main job and this was exactly what he was looking for.

'Archer Finch - The multi billionaire with a mysterious girl.'

He imagined the headline of a tabloid in his head. But the problem was Victor had no idea where to find the two of them again. And so he channeled the stalker inside him, "Think Victor think.. what was a billionaire doing walking the streets of this city. Think!"

And like a flashback, the scene played in his head where he bumped into that girl. Victor remembered that underneath her sweat shirt, that girl was wearing a sports bra. And when Archer came to pick her up, Victor noticed that he was wearing sports shoes.

"So they were there doing something sporty.. what were they doing there? Gym??" Victor was talking aloud to himself and this was freaking out the people sitting around him, "Think you idiot, think!" he yelled at himself, pinching his forehead.

Quickly he started typing in his laptop. He searched for any place around his location where people could go for fitness activities. The results came out with three locations —

1) The Rush — an adventure club

2) Max Gym — a simple gym, and

3) Rick's Dojo — a martial arts school

"I need to check these out," he said packing his laptop back in the bag. People were relieved as he left.

Victor first reached Max Gym. He went to the reception and showed Archer's old picture on his phone, "Hi, I am looking for this person. Does he come to your gym?"

The receptionist was taken aback by Victor's in your face attitude. She looked at the picture and then at Victor. "I am sorry but who are you?"

"You have not seen him here?" Victor shoved the picture in her face again.

"Noo! And please stop trying to reach over the counter," she warned Victor.

Victor did not want to waste his time there and so he walked out. Next stop — Rick's Dojo. As he walked inside, he only saw little kids training in the dojo. A scrawny man with a black belt and karate outfit came up to him with a big smile, "Welcome to Rick's Dojo, May I help you?"

Victory looked around with amazement. "I don't think so!" he said and left quickly.

Minutes later, he was standing at the reception of The Rush. "Hi, I am looking for this person. Does he come to your gym?" Victor repeated the same question.

The receptionist looked at the picture and replied, "We are an adventure club and not a gym. And we do not share the details of our customers with general public."

A big smile appeared on Victor's face, "That's all I wanted to know!"

Victor pocketed his phone and left. Now he started hanging outside The Rush, every day of the week around the time he bumped into Vera. The weekdays did not yield any result, but on Saturday, he hit jackpot.

"Oh yeah!" he cried with joy as he saw Archer and Vera entering the club. Quickly he snapped a few pictures of them and noted the time in his small journal.

"I got you Billionaire!" Victor was really happy.

Chapter 5

Vera and Archer were making regular appearances at The Rush. Together, they observed each other's climbing techniques and improved themselves. Unaware of being stalked by a sociopath with a high end camera, both of them had grown really fond of each other.

"Hey, can I ask you something?" Archer said with a hesitant smile. Vera's gaze told her that she was waiting for his question. "Would you like to go out with me?"

"Aren't we out right now?" Vera knew what Archer meant, but she decided to have a little fun with it. Archer was an expert at sarcasm and he instantly picked up what Vera was doing.

"Let me take you out on a dinner. A proper dinner!" Archer did not beat around the bush this time.

Vera wanted to say yes, but her last date flashed before her eyes. She was not sure whether her mother will unintentionally ruin this date or not. But she did not want to let this opportunity go. "Can I think about it?" she asked.

Archer was not expecting anything other than a yes, and so he was a little surprised.

"Of course!" he said while wondering what could have possibly made Vera have second thoughts about a date.

That day both of them did not talk much like usual and left the Club a little early. Victor noticed this sudden deviation and followed Vera like he did every week. By now, he knew where Vera lived and worked. He was collecting enough juice to make a compelling story.

That night, Vera talked to Jane about what happened earlier.

"You are supposed to say yes, when a handsome guy asked you out." Jane reminded her.

"I wanted to, but you know what Mom did when I went out on my last date." Vera said.

"So you think your Mother will create problems every time you will go out with a guy?"

Vera could see how ridiculous that sounded but she had no justification for her prejudice.

"I don't know, I am not very comfortable. Mom keeps calling me when I am with Archer. What would she do when I go out on a date with him?"

Jane presented a simple solution to her problem, "You know what? You guys plan a date. And I will accompany your mother that evening. We will watch some classics on TV. She likes those, right?"

Vera really liked this idea. She had seen Jane calm down the most irate passengers at the airline desk. There was no way her mother could outwit and outsmart Jane. Suddenly, she was able to see her date with Archer coming through.

"You would do that for me? Really!" Vera asked to confirm.

"Of course I would do that. What are friends for?" Jane replied in a warm tone. "Besides, I will need someone to babysit my kids after I am married. And so consider this as a prep work."

Vera laughed at Jane's scheme, "Your future planning is getting out of hands."

"Wait till you hear about my plans for my divorce." Jane said.

"Divorce? You are planning for your divorce? Who does that?"

"Hey, hope for the best, prepare for the worst!" Jane replied with a smile.

"I got you. I got you!" Vera was laughing.

"So you call the blondie and tell him that he can have the privilege of taking you on a date." Jane reminded Vera.

"Blondie? His name is Archer."

"Do you want me to babysit your mother or not?" Jane asked.

"I will call Blondie right away!"

"Good!"

Vera hung up and dialed Archer's number.

"Hey! Whats up?" his voice cheered Vera even more.

"Remember, you asked if we could go out for a dinner..?" Vera tried to sound innocent.

"That proper dinner? Yeah! You said you need time to think about it."

Vera waited for a second before saying anything, "Well, I would really like to have that proper dinner."

"Awesome! You have any recommendations?" Archer was elated.

"Yes, there is a restaurant that I really like. If you don't mind I would like to show you that place." Vera replied.

Archer was ready to go anywhere with this woman, and Vera was so excited about their date. They decided the time for next week and hung up.

From across the street, Victor captured Vera's smile in his camera as she talked to Archer sitting by her window. "What are you so happy about? Let me guess.." he speculated. "He is taking you on a fancy date."

Victor could sense what was going to happen next.

*****

Vera was wearing a lovely golden dress. This was not from her old wardrobe, but an addition to her new collection. For the first time in years, she was not worried about her mother.

Right now she was on a date and that was the only thing on her mind.

Archer arrived at her place in a limousine. Together they left home while Jane assured Vera that she will take care of her mother. Vera was all set to enjoy this evening.

Together they reached Vera's favorite restaurant. This was an old Italian establishment her father used to take her. But to her surprise, she was not able to recognize this place. Though she was certain it was the restaurant she loved, it looked completely different than how she had remembered it. The old brick building had now turned into a beautiful five star restaurant. Both of them got out of the limousine and entered the restaurant. The main door led them into an elevator that was made of mirrors. The light reflected from the mirrors was illuminating Vera and Archer's eyes. Archer slowly brought his hand close to Vera and grabbed her hand. Soon the door opened — To her astonishment, Vera was now standing on the roof of that restaurant. From here she could see the whole city and beyond its limit. Big mountains sprawled outside the city, surrounding it like a guardian. The waiter showed them there table. They were the only ones there.

Vera and Archer started with a bottle of wine and after dinner they were quite drunk.

"You know, the moment I saw your picture, I fell in love with your hair." Vera confessed.

Archer laughed and came closer to her. "You want to touch my hair?" he offered her. Vera did not pass on this opportunity and moved her fingers through Archer's hair. They were soft and silky like a dream. Vera realized Archer was moving his hand over her thigh. He looked into her eyes for approval, and with a smile, Vera validated his actions.

Slowly, Archer's hand went under Vera's golden dress and now his skin was touching her thigh. Archer's warm hand gave her goosebumps and she grabbed his beautiful hair in a fist. Knowing he was hitting the right notes, Archer then placed his other hand behind Vera's neck and gently brought her face close to his. Their eyes met, and then their lips.

Vera pulled Archer back and they fell in her bed together. Archer was wearing his gym vest and it was drenching with his sweat. Since they started going to the adventure club, Vera had always wanted to feel Archer's broad chest after every sweaty session. And now she was free to do anything she *desired. In one quick motion, Archer took off his gym vest and moved over Vera. He then took off her golden dress really slowly and revealed the red and blue bra inside.*

Vera's hands were working on Archer's trousers and a minute later, he was in his underwear that he took off himself. Vera could see his manhood was ready for her. As she touched it with her shivering hands, she could feel its warmth.

"Fuck Me, Archer!" she said gazing into his blue eyes. Archer obliged to the command of this beautiful woman and pulled her dress up. Inside, she was wearing a matching panties. Slowly, Archer started taking them off while kissing her all over her thighs and legs. This man was making Vera very horny.

He slowly spread her legs and positioned himself in the middle of her thighs. With one hand frisking over her thigh, Archer placed his finger at the entrance of her vagina. His fingers told him that she was more than ready.

With one gentle push, his wet fingers entered her vagina and Vera let out a wild moan. It drove Archer mad with lust and he started fingering Vera, moving his arm back and forth. Vera could feel the extra force of Archer's arm behind his finger.

"Archer, give me the real thing! I want it so badly." Vera pleaded.

Archer took out his finger and leaned over her. They shared a passionate kiss before she grabbed his cock and started stroking it. Feeling how wet his penis was getting, Vera could tell that Archer was now ready. "Take me Archer!" she then commanded him.

Archer placed his dick at the right spot and pushed it forward.

"Ohh Archer!" Vera moaned calling his name. Archer placed his hands under her waist and started pumping her rapidly. To match his strokes, Vera slowly started moving her hips back and forth. Together they matched each other's strokes and created a rhythm.

The grassland around them was bathed in the light of the setting sun and Vera could sense that she was about to reach her peak. "Faster! Faster!" she cried closing her eyes and Archer did what she asked.

Clutching the grass in both her hands Vera cried her lungs out as she exploded inside. But Archer was nowhere near his finish line and he kept fucking her like a wild animal. Vera's loud moans and cries made him mad with lust and he increased his intensity.

Now, Archer picked her up in his arms and placed Vera on his thighs. Her breasts were now facing Archer, with her hard nipples touching his chest. Vera could feel the goosebumps on Archer's skin and by his face she could tell that he was about to finish.

"Yeah baby! Fuck me!" she cried, encouraging Archer. His hands clutched her waist tightly as Archer finished like a firework inside her. She could feel him shooting inside her and she hid his face in her breasts to comfort him.

Both of them stayed like that for some time and then they collapsed on Vera's bed. Vera kept running her fingers through Archer's golden hair and soon they both fell asleep. Vera closed her eyes and the darkness took over her world.

In that darkness a wild earthquake rocked Vera's bed. She looked around and found Archer in her arms. The whole world kept shaking in a rhythm and suddenly, Archer tumbled over the bed and fell off. To Vera's horror the ground opened and swallowed Archer into its dark depth.

Crying his name, she jumped out of the bed. And as she fell from her bed, she found herself falling into a bottomless darkness. "Archer!" she cried his name, but there was nothing for her to see or hear. And then, her back contacted the bottom of this pit.

With a jerk, Vera woke up in her bed. She was sweating all over and found her phone was vibrating, shaking her whole bed. Collecting her wits, she checked her phone and it was her alarm. "Stupid dream!" she said holding her head.

Vera was not sure whether it was a beautiful dream or a nightmare. But with each passing second every memory of that dream kept fading away from her mind. She tried to hold on to one thing or another, but the only thing she was able to keep in her head was Archer's beautiful eyes.

She was happy to have that.

*****

Vera was wearing her blue dress for the date. Jane was standing behind her helping her get ready.

"Babe, this dress looks fabulous on you." Jane smiled with awe.

Vera knew Jane was telling the truth. She had seen a similar compliment in Cyril's eyes when she went on a date with him wearing the same dress.

"Vera, your cab is here." her Mom called from downstairs.

"Coming Mom!" she said looking at herself one more time in the mirror. She then turned to Jane after picking up her purse and phone. "I will be back before 11. You watch a movie with her."

"Stop worrying about me and your mother. I will handle this. You go and enjoy your time with blondie." Vera smiled and pulled Jane towards her. They broke their hug after a few seconds and Vera went downstairs.

Alice looked at her, "This dress looks so good on you."

"Mom you have told me the same thing a thousand times." Vera said kissing her.

"And I will say this a million more times. Now go and have fun!"

Vera smiled at her mother and walked out of the door. She sat in the cab and drove off.

*****

The old Italian restaurant was just like Vera had remembered it. An old brick building with just one story and an old board. Though they have updated their interior, the ambiance was almost the same. Vera entered the restaurant and found Archer waiting for her inside. He stood up on seeing Vera coming his way. She could see the same expressions on Archer's face that Cyril had.

"You look lovely!" Archer said.

No matter how many times Vera had heard it from different people, it still filled her with joy. She then returned Archer's compliment with another one. "You look really good in a suit. You should wear it more often."

"You have no idea!" Archer chuckled. Both of them sat down and started talking.

"My father used to bring us here, me and my mom. He loved Italian food. And so this restaurant holds a special place in my heart."

"Hello Vera!" a young woman greeted her from behind.

"Marissa!" Vera exclaimed looking at her. "How are you?"

"I am good. And feel even better after seeing you here tonight." Marissa was so happy to see her.

Vera introduced Archer to her friend, "Marissa, this is my friend Archer. Archer, Marissa's dad opened this restaurant, and now she is the boss." Archer just smiled and nodded.

"Well you guys enjoy your evening, and I will see you later. I have to go and take care of some delivery issues." Marissa held Vera's hand.

"Alright. I will see you later." Vera said as Marissa walked away.

"Looks like you know them pretty well." Archer said.

"Yes, being a regular for a decade has its perks." Vera smiled. "After my father's death, this is one of those things that made me feel close to him."

Archer did not know how to respond to that and so he just smiled.

"Tell me about your family." Vera wanted to know more about Archer.

"Well," Archer thought of the best possible way to put it out there. "My parents passed away when I was very young and so my mother's sister took me in. She, being quite busy with her life, sent me to a boarding school. After that I earned my degree in Aeronautics and started working."

All this time Vera used to think that her life was hard. Losing her father was the biggest pain of her life, and she had always believed that it was one of the biggest tragedies of her life. But knowing about Archer, her problems seemed like nothing. In that moment, her heart was filled with immeasurable love for Archer.

"You alright?" Archer asked Vera.

Getting off her train of thoughts, Vera remembered that she was on a date. "I am sorry. That would have been so tough. After my father died, we went through some financial hardships, but then I found a job. So I can understand how hard it must have been for you."

Archer wanted to tell Vera that unlike her, he had never experienced financial hardships. His family always had a shitload of money. But keeping quiet about his real identity was taking a mental toll on him. His heart wanted to tell Vera everything, but his brain did not want to lose her. There was a struggle going on inside Archer's body.

"I need to go to the restroom," he excused himself.

Archer locked himself in the restroom and looked into the mirror. "Dammit!" he was frustrated. He was not a liar and so hiding his true identity from Vera was too much for him. He thought of calling Phillip and discuss this. But he knew what Phillip was going to tell him, and so he decided not to call him.

For one good minute, Archer kept staring at his reflection in the mirror. Looking into his own eyes, he remembered what kind of man he was. "She deserves to know and I am going to tell her the truth tonight." Archer was certain of what he wanted to do now.

"Beep-Beep!"

A sharp beep invaded his moment of privacy. Owning several cameras and gadgets, Archer was quickly able to identify that sound — it was a DSLR camera. Quickly, he jumped at the restroom window and saw a human figure running away. "Bastard!" Archer said in frustration.

Victor Cooper was running as fast as he could. Archer had spotted him from the restroom. "How stupid!" he cursed himself for forgetting to silence his camera. His whole operation was now in jeopardy due to one lousy mistake he made.

He had followed Vera from her house to this restaurant where he found Archer with her. He was trying to take some shots of him inside the restroom when this fiasco happened.

Victor quickly turned a corner and appeared on the street. He quickly changed his pace to normal. He did not want people to notice him and so he kept his head low and kept walking. He reached his white scooter that was parked in a corner. A few meters away from the Italian restaurant.

Victor knew that going back to the restaurant was a bad idea. Archer Finch now knew that he was being followed, and so the best option was to get out of there as quickly as possible. Victor knew where to find Vera, and so he knew where to find Archer. Besides, it was Vera he was more interested in. She made this story more appealing.

He checked the pictures from this evening one last time before starting his scooter. The images seemed fine and Victor was relieved.

But suddenly, a cold and strong hand grabbed his neck from the behind and pulled him away from his scooter.

"Motherfucker! I have been noticing you for a long time." Archer grabbed the camera by its lens and pulled it towards himself. "You think I don't know you have been following us to the club?"

"Robbery! Robbery!" Victor started yelling.

In return, Archer cupped his mouth and slammed him into the wall behind him. "One more word from your mouth and I am going to smash your camera against this wall." Archer said in a cold tone.

Victor noticed that with his other hand, Archer was holding his camera. He had enough room to smash the camera into the wall, and so Victor decided to do as he was asked. The camera was expensive and the pictures inside were priceless.

Archer could see that Victor was ready to cooperate and so he took his hand off his mouth and snatched the camera. "Who sent you?"

"What?" Victor did not know how to answer that.

Archer was quickly going through the pictures and what he saw in the camera, made him mad. "You asshole! You are following my girlfriend."

Archer grabbed Victor by his throat. The cameraman was no match for Archer's strong body. His throat felt as if it was being squeezed like a lemon. He tried to speak, but only vowel sounds came out of his mouth.

"I am going to fucking kill you! How dare you go after her?" Archer was turning into the hulk. Victor knew rich people like him did not care about breaking the law. He knew his life was in danger.

He then looked behind Archer and using all the air in his lungs screamed, "Vera! Help me!" Archer quickly turned back expecting Vera behind him, but there was nothing.

Victor hit Archer in the stomach with his knee and pushed him away. Archer lost his balance and fell on the ground. Victor jumped on his scooter and fled.

Archer stood up and dusted his clothes. He now had Victor's camera and all the pictures inside. After checking the pictures in the camera one more time, Archer took out his cellphone and called Phillip.

"Hey there! How is your date going?" Phillip was cheerful.

"Not good Phil! Not good at all."

"What happened? You told her?"

Archer did not know how to break this news to Phillip without sounding like an idiot. Since he started meeting Vera, Phillip had advised him to tell Vera the truth. And now, she was being stalked by a crazy photographer because of him.

"Uhh.. No! I was about to tell her, when something happened."

"What happened?" Phillip sounded serious.

"I caught this photographer outside the restaurant where we came. And his camera is filled with Vera's pictures. This is all my fault."

"How do you know it's because of you?" Phillip asked.

"Because I have spotted this photographer a couple of times before. He keeps taking our photos together and now I am looking at these pictures of Vera at her house. This asshole followed her from her house to this restaurant."

"Archer, we still don't know whether he is doing this because she is dating you, or because he is a creepy stalker following Vera. So just calm down and think for a moment. The first thing you need to do is tell Vera everything and drop her home right now."

Archer knew Phillip was right, but telling Vera the truth right now felt like a bad idea for their relationship. "I will drop her home and come back. Lets talk about it then."

"Alright!" Phillip said and hung up.

Archer walked to his car and threw the camera under his seat. He then returned to the restaurant. He first went back to the restroom and fixed himself.

Then he returned to the restaurant, but looking at Vera, his heart bent his brain to its will. Instead of ending the date early, he enjoyed the evening, like they had planned.

In the end, Archer dropped Vera home and bid her goodbye.

Ecstatic and oblivious, Vera entered entered her home.

Chapter 6

In the morning, Vera thanked Jane for keeping her mother entertained behind her back.

"Don't mention it." Jane said wearing her shoes, "You know why I am doing this."

"Yes, and consider me a babysitter for your future kids." Vera said.

"So before I leave, tell me how it went? You seemed so happy last night I did not want to poke you." Jane was so eager to know all the details.

Vera pulled out a chair and sat down in front of her. "It was so amazing! To be honest, I was not expecting everything to go as planned. When he went to the bathroom, for some reason my heart kept telling me that some fuck up was taking place. And when I was about to give up, he came back. So that was the big suspense of my date."

"What happened then?" Jane opened her eyes wide.

"Well, we talked about our families. Well my family, his family died when he was a little boy." Vera remembered.

"Wow!" Jane exclaimed, "You have got yourself a Bruce Wayne."

"Bruce Wayne is a billionaire!" Vera corrected her friend and continued — "So I told him about Mom, and you, and my college life and he told me about his school life and how he got a degree in aeronautics." Vera was picturing Archer in that suit from last night. It was giving her goosebumps and making her wet at the same time.

Jane was able to read her friend's state. "Hey, stop lusting around and give me more details. Until now it's just regular stuff. Did you guys do anything?"

Vera let out a sigh, "No. We did nothing. He got a call from work and so he seemed in a rush to go back. He said he had to go home and work on something."

"Dude seems busy! So you guys didn't even make out?" Jane wondered.

"If I remember correctly, last time you reminded me to keep my hands off on first dates." Vera argued in her favor.

"I said not to jump in the sack on first date. There is no rule that says you should not make out with your date." Jane countered.

"I tried, but he seemed a little pre-occupied. So I did not try hard."

"Fine! But now what?" Jane asked curiously.

"We will continue our arrangement. Meeting at the club every Saturday and I guess a date every once in a while." Vera was smiling just thinking of it.

But Jane suddenly turned serious, "Okay, and what if you guys really like each other? You think you can get serious with him?"

Vera knew why Jane was asking this question, but she remained quiet.

"Are you ready to get married?" Jane asked again.

"I don't know if he wants to get married." Vera replied.

"Don't talk like a child. What if he asks you to marry him one day? What are you going to tell him?" Jane looked at Vera for answers but she kept her lips sealed.

"Tell me!" Jane cried. "Will you tell him that you cannot marry him or anybody else because you need to take care of your mother?"

"Please stop! I don't want to think about it right now. Things are finally going my way and I don't want to ruin them."

Jane could hear the sadness in Vera's voice and so she stopped. Both of them sat in the room without saying anything.

Outside the door, Alice stood with a tray of breakfast in her hands. She did not know what to do — she just realized she was keeping her daughter chained. Slowly, she turned around without making a sound and went back to her room.

Almost falling in her bed, Alice wondered what she could do to make her daughter free of her burden. Vera was close to her father and so she rarely talked about her problems to her mother. And now Alice did not know what to do in this situation.

But then, she remembered something. She stood up and opened her wardrobe. Going back to her bed, she brought a small stool with her and placed it before the open wardrobe. Standing on the stool, Alice looked in the corner of the top shelf. Covered in dust and darkness, there was a small box placed in one corner. Alice pulled the box out and sat down in her bed.

She remembered the day when Michael brought this box to the house. "This, is my promise to you," he said to her that day. "I am going to put money in this box and once we have enough, I am going to take you around the world."

Alice wiped the dust off the box with her hands and opened it. It was teeming with money.

"How did I forget about this?" she asked herself. But her eyes noticed something else inside the box — it was an old paper folded neatly. Its faded off-white color made it stand out among all the dollar bills. Alice picked the paper up and un-folded it. It was a note from her dead husband —

"My lovely Alice,

I am saving this money for us to see the world, but life does not come with a warranty. I don't know what is going to happen tomorrow and so if it comes to a point when only one of us is left to use this money, I suggest we spend it like it's never going to end. If you are reading this note without me, go out and see the world without me. And if I am reading this note without you by my side, only God can tell you how much I miss you.

Love,

Michael."

A teardrop fell over that letter.

*****

A week went by and Vera came back from another date with Archer. While heading towards her room, she heard her mother from behind, "Vera!"

"Yes Mom," she turned around and looked at her.

"Do you really like this man you have been dating?" Alice asked.

Vera had no idea why she was being asked something like this by her mother. But she kept her straight face on, "I guess so. Why are you asking this?"

"If everything goes right, will you think of marrying him?" Alice shot another round.

Vera was not able to understand why her mother was suddenly interested in her affair. But deep down she was getting the idea that her mother was going to ask her about her life choices.

"Mom, I am really tired right now. Can we discuss it in the morning?" Vera quickly turned around and went to her room. Alice stood in the main hall and then went back to her room.

The next morning, Vera came down and did not find her mother. She looked through the whole house, but Alice had disappeared.

Putting on a jacket, Vera went out and looked around the neighborhood, but there was no sign or trace of her mother anywhere. Tired, she came back home after spending an hour outside. Coming back home, Vera started feeling worried. She thought of calling her relatives, but stopped herself. "I should check her room first."

Vera entered her mother's room and realized that something was missing. And it was not her mother, but something else. Something that was a part of this room, but now was gone. And then she saw it, her mother's favorite black suitcase was gone. It had left a mark in the corner where it protected the wall from dust. Vera's heart sank and she collapsed on the bed. "Fuck!" Tears came out of her eyes and she felt terrible about snubbing her last night. But then she collected herself and went to the main hall. Her mother did not carry a cell-phone and so she was not sure what to do next.

She decided to call Jane and tell her about it, but then Vera noticed something on the table. It was an empty soda can, placed upside down on the table. She took a closer look at it and found a paper underneath it with her name.

Quickly, Vera opened the paper and started reading —

"Dear Vera,

I know what you have been going through after your father's death. You left your life and future to care for me and now I am seeing you in this horrible dilemma where you will have to choose between a good life for yourself or getting stuck with me. And I am not the kind of mother who will let her child suffer.

Please don't worry about me. I have enough money to take care of myself. I plan to enjoy myself and suggest you do the same. It's about time, and I am going for that holiday your father promised me.

I love you my dear.

Mom.

PS: This is not a suicide note. I am not going to kill myself."

Vera broke down. All this time she thought her mother had no idea about her problems. But it turned out, she took all the blame upon herself and removed herself out of the situation. She put the letter down, wiped her tears and called Jane.

"Jane, Mom left!" she cried.

Jane was not able to understand what Vera meant. "What do you mean?" she asked.

Vera explained the whole thing to her and even read the letter. She was crying all the time.

"You stay there, I am coming." Jane said and hung up.

Within an hour, both of them were sitting together.

"Should we go to the police? File a missing complaint?" Vera asked.

"I don't know. Your mother left on her own will. So technically, she is not missing. I am not sure how the cops are going to look at it." Jane said taking a deep breath. "Lets just calm down for a minute and put our heads together. We need to fig-ure out where she must have gone."

Vera picked up her phone and started dialing.

"Who are you calling?" Jane asked.

"Archer!" she replied.

*****

Archer was playing golf that morning when his phone rang.

"Hey Vera. How are you?" his face lit up answering the call.

"Archer, my mother left the house. I don't know where she is." Vera was crying.

Archer realized how serious this was. He signaled Phillip to come with him in a corner. After making sure nobody was able to hear them, Archer put the phone on speaker and started talking to Vera —

"Vera, do you have any idea why she left?" Archer's tone was firm like a detective.

Vera felt obliged to tell him everything, and so she started narrating everything in chronological order. Archer had heard much of that stuff on their first date, but now he was getting to know Vera's dilemma.

"Wow!" Archer said to himself but then composed his voice. "Listen to me, she wrote she is going on that holiday that your father promised her. Tell me, where was he going to take her?"

Vera wiped her tears and read the letter again. "He used to say that they would go around the world in a ship."

"Okay, we are getting somewhere. Now tell me, does your mother have enough money to go around the world?" Archer asked another question.

"I don't know. She does have some bank accounts of her own but we are not that rich." Vera remembered.

"Okay, now tell me, when did she leave?"

Vera tried to remember but she did not come up with anything, "I woke up at 8 and she was already gone. I am guessing she took off way before that."

"Alright, you stay at home, in case she comes back and I will make some calls. I have a friend who knows some people."

"Could you please come here?" Vera cried.

"Let me take care of this and I will be with you. Okay?" Archer said.

Vera hung up and Archer looked at Phillip. Archer did not need to say anything. Phillip took out his phone and made some calls.

"Hey, I need details of her mother — her name, address, picture." Phillip asked Archer while talking to somebody on the phone. Archer called Vera and got all the necessary information emailed to him. He then forwarded that to Phillip.

After relaying from one person to another, Phillip finally had something, "I think we found her," he said to Archer.

*****

Archer, Vera and Phillip reached the bay and boarded their yacht.

"Who is this guy?" Vera asked Archer looking at Phillip who was busy with his phone all the time.

"He is my friend I told you about? Very influential guy." Archer replied.

"Is this his yacht?" she asked.

"Uhh.. yeah! It's his.." Archer said looking at Phillip.

Hours later, they were able to see a cruise ship at a distance. "There!" Archer said. "Your mother is on that cruise."

Vera could not believe it. Her mother had left her to go on a cruise.

Vera, Archer and Phillip boarded the cruise from the yacht and the captain himself took them to the lounge where his passengers were enjoying a post lunch variety show.

"MOM!" Vera screamed at her mother in the spectators. The program abruptly stopped and Vera walked to her mother with heavy steps. "What were you thinking?" she yelled at the top of her voice.

"Ooohh!" Phillip giggled standing by Archer.

"Do you have any idea what you did to me today?" Vera continued yelling. A few attendants arrived on the scene. "Miss, I need you to calm down," a female attendant warned Vera.

Phillip signaled Archer to do something.

And so, he walked to the scene with the captain. "Can we get these two a room, where they can have their discussion in private?" Archer looked at the captain.

After much walking, Archer, led Vera and Alice inside a first class cabin. "I will be waiting outside," he said closing the door behind him.

"How dare you leave me like this?" Vera screamed.

"I left you? You only live with me. But you have left me long ago." Alice spoke out. "Whenever I try to talk to you about your future, you dismiss me like a child. I am tired of being treated like that. After you go to your job, I stay in that house all alone. How dare you lecture me for leaving you? At least I never ran away from a discussion."

"But why did you pull this stunt? You could have clearly told me instead of leaving like this." Vera was still furious.

"Oh please! Have you forgotten how many times I tried to talk to you. And don't expect me to beg you to have a conversation with me. I am your mother and I deserve much better than that." Alice was now letting her anger out.

"But it's my life, and my future. Why do you keep pushing me to make a choice? Things were going so good for me and you went and did _this_!"

"I did _this_??" Alice screamed in astonishment. "I gave up my life for you and your father. I toiled with him when we struggled for money. I put his and your needs before mine all my life. At least you have Jane to talk to. Do you know who do I have to talk to?? NOBODY!"

Alice's anger had trumped Vera's and now she was just listening to her mother.

"Your father was a private man and never told me how he really felt. He kept it all inside him and maybe that is why his heart gave up. And then you grew up to be just like him — you never came to me to talk. All you did was sit in your room and be alone. Try to understand, it's your right to be alone, but when you do that in a house with two people, you are not giving the other person a choice. For your selfishness, you and your father left me alone! Tell me what wrong I did by coming here? Tell me honestly, If you go back right now and resume your life like normal, would it stop without me?"

That made Vera think. She had made her mother obsolete. Vera realized that though she regularly cried about sacrificing her future to take care of her mother, she was actually not doing anything for her. It was not her mother who was holding her back — she was doing it to herself.

The realization was too heavy for Vera to take in. She sat down in a chair and looked at the floor. Tears broke out of her eyes and ran down her cheeks.

Alice could not stop herself anymore. After all she was a mother.

"Oh my baby!" she wrapped her arms around Vera.

"I am sorry mother!" Vera held her mother tightly.

Both of them embraced each other.

*****

Phillip nudged Archer, signaling him to turn around.

Archer saw Alice and Vera coming out of the cabin.

"Mom, this is Archer, and his friend Phillip," Vera introduced her mother to Archer for the first time.

"It's a pleasure meeting you, Ma'am!" Archer shook her hand, but Alice pulled him towards herself and gave him a tight hug. "Thank you for bringing my daughter to me."

"Mom, it was because of Phillip." This was Vera's way of thanking Phillip. "He brought us here in his yacht."

"You own a yacht? You must be rich!" Alice joked thanking him.

Phillip looked at Archer, "I believe I am, Mrs Jones."

Archer's grin signaled Phillip to stay quiet.

"So what do we do now?" Phillip ask.

"Lets go back, Mrs Jones!" Archer looked at Alice.

"I think I will stay here. I like this ship. Besides, I deserve this holiday." Alice replied. She really did not want to go. It was the first day of the cruise and she was enjoying it, until Vera barged in.

Archer looked at Vera who in turn looked at her mother, "Mom, are you sure?"

"Yes! You guys go ahead, I will be back when this ship comes back."

"I guess they are not going to refund your money, so your better enjoy." Vera smiled.

Before leaving the cruise, Archer made all the arrangements for Vera to communicate with Alice any time. Bidding farewell to her mother, Vera left the cruise with Archer and Phillip.

*****

"Look at this." Vera said looking outside the yacht window. "This morning, my life was upside down. My mother had left home and I had no idea what to do." She turned to Archer who was standing behind him, "And now I am in a million dollar yacht."

"And I have no one but you to thank for this, Archer!" her eyes were filled with tears.

Archer just stared at Vera in disbelief. He had developed feelings for Vera way before their first date took place. But he did not want to open himself up before telling her the truth. "Don't cry Vera. I will always be there for you…" Archer wanted to say a lot more, but Vera could not wait anymore. She pulled Archer close and planted a kiss on his lips.

Forgetting to measure time, they kissed each other passionately. Vera pushed Archer against the wall and he lifted her in his arms. Vera suddenly, pulled her face away.

"Is Phillip expecting you?" she asked.

"What? No!" Archer replied almost laughing.

"Great!" Vera kicked the door closed that locked itself from inside. And then she grabbed Archer like she was a lioness and he was her prey. Archer could feel her nails going deep in his skin through his shirt.

"What has gotten into you?" he smiled as Vera seductively looked at him. Both of them were hungry for each other's flesh. Archer jumped at her this time, grabbing her in his arms. He picked her up and threw her on the bed.

Quickly, he unbuttoned his shirt and threw it away. Vera was finally able to touch that chiseled chest outside of her dream. "Come here!" she growled and grabbed him from the ribs. She started planting kisses on Archer's chest while he took off her top.

Now it was Archer's turn to return the favor. He took off Vera's bra and cupped her round breasts in his hands. Like a child, he lunged at them with his mouth and started sucking on them. With each lick and kiss on her breasts, Vera could feel her panties getting more and more wet. While her moans filled the cabin, Archer worked on her jeans. As he released her legs from the prison of her denims, Archer used both his hands to rub her vagina from over her underwear.

Guiding with just one hand, Vera put Archer's hand inside her underwear. She led him to the right spot and indicated for him to rub her. She was quite lubricated down there and Archer faced no problem in putting his fingers inside. Where his mouth was sucking her breasts, his fingers were working on Vera's vagina. Suddenly, Vera was able to remember her dream. She could remember everything now, but that dream did not feel as good as this moment. Her back was arching due to the overwhelming pleasure.

After a violent session of rubbing, Archer felt a warm gush of liquid coming out of Vera's vagina. "Oh Archer!" she cried while ejaculating. Archer left her breasts and kissed her on her beautiful lips.

Vera cuddled with Archer while kissing his chest and neck. And then she started unbuttoning his trousers. After taking his pants off, Vera slid down his underwear and his erect cock jumped out like a tensed spring.

It was way bigger than she had imagined in her dreams. Besides its length, its girth impressed Vera and she wanted to eat it up. Grabbing it with both her hands she took it in her mouth and started massaging it with her lips and tongue. Archer spread his back on the bed and closed his eyes. Now Vera was starting to feel horny again and so she climbed over the bed and placed her vagina over Archer's face. Forming a Sixty-Nine position, now both of them were pleasuring each other.

Vera kept both sucking and pumping Archer's dick wildly. And when Archer felt he was about to cum, he pushed Vera away. Vera knew what it meant and so she decided to give her man a break. Getting her face closer to his, Vera planted several deep kisses on his lips. Their naked bodies rubbed against each other on that comfortable bed.

Archer could feel that he was ready and so he placed Vera by his side. Lying behind her he raised one of her legs in the air and placed his cock at the entrance of her pussy.

"Shall I?" he whispered in her eyes for permission.

"Go ahead!" she said.

Archer started fucking Vera from her side. Vera used her hand to rub her clitoris while getting fucked by Archer. Her vagina was doing double time, giving her immense pleasure.

After fucking her in that position for minutes, Archer changed their posture and put her over him. With her face towards Archer and her legs around his waist, Vera bobbed up and down quickly. Archer's cock was glistening with Vera's liquid.

Soon, her legs started getting tired and so Archer grabbed her by her waist. He started rocking her back and forth. Vera understood the basic principle of this position and leaned on her hands after planting them on Archer's chest. She kept fucking Archer until she felt she was about to cum again. She thought of delaying her climax but saw Archer's face. He was about to achieve orgasm and so Vera went to town with that pussy on his dick.

Moments later, both of them exploded together. Vera could feel Archer shooting inside her, and Archer was feeling Vera's warm ejaculation all over her shaft and crotch.

Convulsing and moaning, Vera collapsed over Archer's broad chest. He caught her in his arms and kissed her passionately. Together, they stayed like that and fell asleep.

Chapter 7

Archer dropped Vera home. Both of them shared a passionate kiss at Vera's doorstep. It seemed like Archer still had some fire left in him from the yacht. He pushed Vera against her door and pressed his body against her. Knowing that their neighbors might see them, Vera pushed him away. She kissed him one more time before letting him go. Not wanting to go, Archer walked away from Vera's home and left in his car. Feeling on top of the world Vera looked at Archer's car as it disappeared at the end of the road.

Smiling ear to ear, Vera unlocked her door and stepped inside.

From the rooftop of a building that had a clear view of Vera's home, Victor Cooper was shooting all this. He checked his camera and now he had a clear evidence of billionaire Archer Finch dating an ordinary airline clerk.

"That rich asshole won't know what hit him." Victor was really proud of his latest assignment.

*****

Phillip walked out of a small cafe after his lunch. He checked his phone as it buzzed. Archer was asking him to come home. After typing a reply, Phillip pocketed his phone and stopped at a news stand. A delivery boy dropped a pile of an afternoon tabloid in front of the stand owner. Opening the fresh stock, the owner placed the first pile of that tabloid right in front of Phillip. And what Phillip saw on the front page of that tabloid froze every drop of blood in his body.

"BILLIONAIRE ROMANCES AN ORDINARY GIRL" the head-line was sticking over a big picture of Archer kissing Vera at her door.

"Fuck me!" Phillip said picking up a copy. He dropped a $5 bill and started running.

*****

"Hey, high resolution of each image costs extra. Besides make sure to renew your license next week. I am going to sue you if you use these images without renewing my license. I am the sole owner of these babies." Victor was growling over the phone. He was haggling with a tabloid liaison over the prices of his images.

Suddenly, the Archer-Vera story was spreading like wildfire. All the tabloids were highly interested in this fairy tale story. Before evening, every tabloid wanted a piece of this story. And the only way to run it was to get the images from Victor Cooper. Cooper was sitting on a goldmine.

Random micro blogging sites over the internet stole the images and stories from the tabloids and published them. "*This modern age fairy tale romance will make you believe in love again*" kind of headlines appeared like sprouts all over the web. Suddenly Archer Finch and Vera Jones were internet sensation. Their story was first picked up by low level news channel who mostly ran old clips from youtube as news. They contacted Victor and acquired the rights for a few images that postulated the story of an ordinary girl finding a rich real life prince as a lover.

*****

Vera was having another busy day at work. Passengers were lining up in front of their desk. This time it was the airline's fault. Craving for a maintenance, the systems finally gave up and went down. The management however decided to hush the story from the top brass and pushed low level clerks like

Jane and Vera to bear the brunt. The airline staff was not able to access the passenger information and it was creating a riot like situation at their desk.

"We need a strong diversion. Or these people are going to eat us alive!" Jane told Vera who had no time to look around.

"I am so sorry sir, but our systems are on a scheduled maintenance. We are not able to access any information. But we are holding all our flights till we get back online." Vera tried to explain to one passenger.

"Why don't you just say this is another ridiculous way of your airline to delay our flights. Just because you are the cheapest doesn't give you the right to torture your customers," the man screamed at Vera.

Vera did not want to argue, but she had no response other than, "I am sorry sir!"

It was mandatory for Vera and her colleagues to apologize to the customers in case they faced any inconvenience. But this meaningless apology usually ended up annoying most of the customers. However, the airline maintained its stand over the apology and demanded it from its employees that they follow the proper protocol.

Vera and Jane were apologizing to one customer after another. With each passing minute the customers were growing angrier. A lot of them were demanding a refund, to which Vera and Jane received no response from their upper management.

"Damn you!" a passenger yelled. "I need to be in Detroit by tonight. Give me my money back so that I can take another flight from a decent airline."

"Sir, if you could wait a little longer, I can check your flight information." Jane tried to convince the passenger, but he was not in the mood.

"Fuck you lady! Fuck you!" he stormed off after showing Jane his middle finger.

"We need a miracle to save our asses." Jane cried looking at Vera.

And suddenly, something happened.

"Hey lady, is this you?" A passenger came up to the desk and shoved his phone in Vera's face. An internet article was showing Vera kissing Archer on her door. "A BILLION DOLLAR RO-MANCE" was the headline. Vera could not identify herself, but Archer's golden hair instantly reminded her that it was them. She quickly scanned the article and received a shock when she read the line — "Multi billionaire Archer Finch is dating an airline clerk Vera Jones…"

Jane noticed Vera freezing with shock and she took the phone from her hands. She instantly realized how Vera must have been feeling. And then, one after another many passengers started checking their phones.

Several voices raised the questions similar to "Hey lady, is this really you?"

Vera did not know how to answer them because even she was hearing it for the first time. She had no idea she was dating a billionaire.

The TV in the lounge started playing the news story about Vera and Archer. The passengers forgot about their ordeal and started taking pictures of Vera at her desk.

"Hey, stop taking pictures!" Jane yelled at them, shielding Vera from the flashes of countless phone cameras. Vera's pictures were doing rounds on social media. The passengers who were yelling at her a minute ago were now posting their selfies with Vera in the background.

The TV was playing their news story in a loop. All the channels were doing it. Archer and Vera were trending as Number 1 on twitter and Instagram.

"Why did he hide it from me?" Vera asked Jane who was busy fending the passengers off of her friend.

"I don't know. Maybe he is not serious about you." Jane replied.

Vera was not willing to believe that. She had seen Archer's eyes. They told her he was in love with her as much as she was with him.

"It can't be!" Vera said, "I know he loves me."

"Has he told you that?" Jane asked.

"What?"

"That he loves you. Has he said that to you, ever?" Jane explained.

Vera played all the memories of her and Archer together, but there was no moment in which Archer confessed his love to her.

"Well?" Jane was waiting for an answer. "Sir, please don't reach over the counter. Security!" she yelled out loud.

Vera was now starting to believe Jane. Was Archer only playing with her? Then why did he take all the pains of finding her mother? Why did he ask his friend to lend him his yacht? And then it hit her — It was his yacht. *He* was his powerful friend who found out where her mother was. Vera was thankful to Archer but she did not understand why he hid his real identity from her. She knew she was not a gold digger, and she still did not want any part of Archer's infinite wealth. The only thing she wanted was a beautiful future where the two of them would be together forever.

"I don't know why he did that." Vera covered her face with her hands.

"I will tell you why he did that.." Jane came up with another theory. "He did not trust you. These rich folks have serious trust issues. I read that in some magazine."

The people were gathering to catch a glimpse of Vera as she sat behind the counter. Jane was still playing the bouncer for her friend, keeping the unwanted photographers at bay. Seeing the brewing trouble, the Duty Manager came out and the first thing he did was lashing out at Jane and Vera. "Why are you sitting her? We have customers rioting at our desk and you guys are playing besties? Handle these people and calm them down."

"Do you even know what is going on?" Jane snapped back at the Manager, "You think these people are rioting against our pathetic service? Take a look at that and tell me why she should stand before these crazy people?"

Jane pointed her finger towards a TV in the lounge. The Duty Manager saw the news piece about Vera and Archer. As the reality dawned upon him, Jane found him frozen in his spot.

"Tell me now!" Jane said to the Manager. "What should we say to these men? Better go inside and call the airport security."

The Duty Manager looked at Vera and walked inside the door with slow and steady steps.

Minutes later the airport security arrived and contained the passengers. Finally, Vera had some peace to think. Jane sat by her side and offered her some water.

*****

"What did I tell you that night?" Phillip slammed the tabloid on the table. Archer did not need to look at it. Because by the time Phillip had reached home, their story was all over the media. Archer knew Phillip was going mad and so he thought it was best not to add fuel to the fire by arguing. He knew he was at fault and did not try to defend himself. But Phillip needed to vent his anger out, and he used his words to do that.

"I was hoping you would use your brain and tell that girl who you really were. But you wanted to play the prince and pauper so bad that you fucked it all up." Phillip started pacing around the room, "When you caught that photographer that night, you were sure that he was after Vera because of you. I did not believe that at the moment, but I told you to reveal your identity to your girlfriend. You ignored my advice not once but many times and now you are looking at the consequences."

Phillip took a deep breath and lowered his voice, "If you don't know already then let me inform you that our shares are taking a hit because of this story. Our investors did not like their CEO romancing with an airline clerk. We say not to judge a book by its cover, but we live in a different reality."

"What do you want me to do now?" Archer finally spoke.

"I want you to fix this right now." Phillip replied.

"Do you want me to beat that photographer? Fine, I am going to do that right away." Archer banged his fist into his palm. Phillip stared at Archer with astonishment.

"How big a fool are you to talk like that? You are not supposed to even touch that guy now. It will be really bad for business and your relationship. I want you to come clean before that girl if you really care about her. And leave that asshole to me. I will take care of him."

Archer remembered that he needed to talk to Vera about it. He dialed Vera's number and waited to hear her voice.

"Hello!" Vera answered the phone. Archer could hear that she had been crying.

"Vera, where are you?" he asked.

"Oh, now you care?"

"Don't talk like that. Of course I care for you."

As she wiped her tears, anger took her over. "Then why did you hide it from me?"

Archer knew there was no use of answering that question and so he stayed mum.

"I understand why you did not tell me during our first meetings, but why did you hide it after we grew so close? Were you worried I would eat through all your money? After all, you rich guys think girls like me are gold diggers. Or you were just planning to discard me after having your fun?"

"What are you talking about Vera? I am calling you right now. What does this tell you?" Archer tried to put some sense into Vera, but she was not ready to listen.

"I know why you are calling me. I am not just a dumb airline clerk as you might think. I can understand that this story will be affecting your business and now you need some good PR. Is this your PR call, tell me?" Vera roared like a wounded lioness.

Archer had no answer to that allegation. He knew that if it was him in Vera's position, even he would not have believed himself.

"Vera, please try to understand. I made a terrible mistake and now all I want is you to be with me. I just want to make things right now. Please, please forgive me." Archer was now pleading.

"Do you know at work, people were treating me like I was a fucking animal in a zoo. Taking pictures, gawking and saying the meanest things possible. *Hey what did you do to catch his attention?* Like I am some gold digging whore. Will you make *that* right?"

Again, Archer was speechless. But this time before he could say anything, Vera hung up on him. He tried calling her again, but she rejected his call. Archer knew that she was not going to answer his call.

He got up and looked at Phillip who was staring at him.

"I need to go and meet her."

Phillip nodded, "You go there and I will take care of this photographer."

Archer patted Phillip's shoulder and walked out of the room.

After much thinking, Phillip dialed a number on his phone. "Yeah. I need to find a man. Should be pretty easy to find right now. Hell, let me give you his number and he will tell you his location himself."

*****

"It has been quite an ordeal. At first I thought they were just having fun, but then I saw that spark between them." Victor said sitting in a news studio. A small news channel had invited him to talk about his pictures that were going viral.

"We have Mr Victor Cooper with us in the studio. The man behind the images that showed us the fairy tale love story between multi billionaire Archer Finch and an airline clerk Vera Jones." The news anchor addressed the camera and then she turned towards Victor. "So Mr Cooper, for how long have you been involved in this story?"

"Thank you for calling me here Felicity. It's an honor." Victor showed his polite side before the camera. "Like any photojournalist involved in any project, I invested a lot of my time in this story. And besides my time, this story had taken my sweat, money and blood in equal parts."

"Ooh blood!" the news anchor's eyes twinkled at the mention of the word *blood.* "Tell us more about that."

"Of course," Victor showed his teeth. "It was a cold night when I was sitting outside a restaurant. I knew that Archer and Vera were regulars there and so I was waiting outside in the cold, minding my own business. And before I could even take a picture Archer Finch walked up to me and punched me in the nose."

"Wow! That must have hurt," the news anchor stated the obvious.

"Like a hammer." Victor continued. "I pleaded with him to stop, but he was too drunk."

"Did you hear that?" the news anchor turned to the camera with a horrified expression on her face. "Archer Finch allegedly attacked a man under the influence of alcohol. Tell me Mr

Cooper," she turned back to him, "Were you taking any pictures of him or Miss Jones at that time?"

"Absolutely not. As I said I only took pictures when they were in public areas. I knew they were going to be there for their dinner and so I was waiting for them to come out. But as Archer Finch saw me and my camera, he started attacking me. He broke my camera and destroyed my expensive gear."

"Did you file a police complaint?" the news anchor asked.

Victor laughed, "He is a multi billionaire. And I am a small time photojournalist. It was a cold night when nobody was watching. You really think the cops would have helped me?"

"It certainly is an interesting debate Mr Cooper. Can a billionaire consider himself above the law after having a few drinks? We will discuss this story with Mr Cooper after these commercials." The program cut to the commercials.

The lounge at the cruise was filled with elderly people who were very interested in that story. "Fuck this guy! He seems like a cheap whore with a camera. If her mother was being mugged, he would have photographed it instead of saving her," a guy yelled.

"How do you know?" a woman asked him.

"Oh I can vouch for that billionaire kid. He is such a nice boy. I am telling you he is not a brat who would hit people after getting drunk." Alice said holding her drink.

"How do you know?" the same woman asked her too.

"I know him. He is dating my daughter." Alice said casually.

The woman and old man shared a surprised look. "Is that airline clerk you daughter?"

Alice took a sip from her drink, "Yeah, Vera Jones is my daughter. And that billionaire boy is Archer. He brought my daughter to meet me here on this cruise via a yacht."

"Ohh I remember it," another old man jumped in. "I saw you and your daughter fighting that day." Suddenly, all the old timers recalled the moment when Vera and Alice had a heated argument in the main lounge.

"Yeah, I remember your daughter. Now she looked like she could punch someone," the old man laughed after that. Alice did not feel offended and shared the laughter.

"So is it true? Are they dating?" a voice asked.

"Are they going to marry each other?" another one asked.

"How rich is that fellow?"

Many similar questions kept coming up. Alice could not make out what she was hearing and so she raised her hands and yelled at the top of her voice.

"Quiet!" The noise magically simmered down and Alice started talking again.

"What my daughter and that rich boy do is their own business. I am her mother and am not worried about it. Then why should you or anybody else? We are here on this cruise to have fun and that is the only thing we should be concerned about."

Alice's speech was met with approving hollers and cheers.

"Fuck that photographer!" a sound came from the photographer.

Alice settled down in her seat. "You know what?" the old man said. "I am going to get you a drink. It's on me."

And soon, Alice was being offered drinks and pastries from several companions on the cruise. The news had turned her into a celebrity.

Chapter 8

Victor and Felicity were chatting between the segments. "Listen sweetheart! I am supposed to be on another show in an hour. Could you please wrap up my segment a little quicker? And please do plug in my website as promised."

Felicity smiled and nodded. But as she turned away, her face turned as if she had tasted a bitter fruit. The make up man came close to her face for a quick touch up, "It this what this channel has come to? Interviewing cheap camera whores like him?"

The make up man smiled and went away. The show went back on air and Victor kept talking about how much he invested in this 'story'.

Getting out of the studio, Victor reached the other show that was being shot close to the first one. They asked the same questions and he gave the same answers. But this time, he also implied that his divine intervention played a huge part in bringing these two together. "You see, in a way, without me, they would not have been together." Victor blew his own trumpet on that show. Between the commercial break, he received another phone call asking for him to appear on another show. Victor told them that he was already doing one show and so it wouldn't be possible for him to be there. The show runners offered to pick him up and Victor told them his location.

Waiting outside the studio, Victor was growing impatient. He received another phone call.

"Yeah. Of course you can have them. That is why I made those pictures. Its $500 for one picture and you get a 1 week license." The caller haggled about the price and Victor laughed him off. "The price went up buddy. I just did two TV shows and so my pictures are now a little costlier."

The caller tried to convince Victor to come back to his original price, but the man knew his pictures were worth more than what they used to be. "That is my final offer my friend. Call me if you are willing to pay up."

As Victor hung up, a station wagon pulled up in front of him across the street.

"Mr. Cooper?" the driver asked.

"About damn time." Victor said walking towards the vehicle.

The car took Victor in and drove off.

*****

Archer reached the airport he could see the news channels running his story. And seeing Victor's face on the screen was making his blood boil. But he focused on why he was here. With quick steps he walked towards Vera's airline desk.

As he reached the desk, he was stopped by the security.

"Sorry sir! But the desk has been temporarily closed. You will be notified about your flight's status."

"I am not a passenger. I am here to meet somebody in the airline." Archer explained himself. But the guard was not willing to let Archer go through.

"There is no way I am going to let you pass Sir. The passengers almost rioted in this area and so now it's a sensitive area that is to be kept free of any passenger or possible rioter."

"Do I look like a rioter to you? And I told you I am not a passenger." Archer said.

The guard stared at his face, "I am sorry sir, but I will need you to go back. This area is temporarily closed."

Archer knew that arguing with this guard was not going to take him anywhere. He took his phone and started calling Vera. But as the phone rang, Vera rejected the call. The guard stared at Archer's face as he frustratingly took the phone off his ear.

"Try to understand it's very important that I go there and talk to my girlfriend. She is very depressed right now."

Another guard arrived at the spot and took a good look at Archer's face. "Hey..!! You are that billionaire guy. Aren't you?"

Though he did not want to, Archer smiled for this guard.

"Hey, this is the guy man!" The new guard told the old one and showed him the TV screen. They were showing Archer and Vera's pictures on the program.

"Wow! You are a billionaire," the guard wondered. "And yet you were standing before me, asking me to let you through."

"Uhh, yeah!" Archer said.

"Well I am sorry man. I didn't know it was you. You deserve to go and meet your girlfriend," the new guard said and let Archer go. With no time to waste, Archer quickly walked past those guards.

"Hey stop," the old guard commanded Archer from behind.

Slowly, he turned around, "What?"

"Can we have a selfie with you man?" the old guard asked very politely.

Archer obliged with the request and after the selfie he was running to the desk. But he found that the desk was empty and so he knocked on the door to the employee entrance.

"Yes?" a pair of eyes peeped through a hole.

"Hello, I am here to see Vera Jones." Archer replied.

"Holy shit! It's you!" the eyes said with a shock. "Wait!"

The door opened and the eyes now had a full face. It was an African American man with short hair. As Archer tried to enter, he blocked his way.

"I am sorry, I cant let you in. Airport regulations. No civilian is allowed inside. But I will call Vera right here. My name is Frankie by the way."

Frankie turned around and yelled, "Hey Vera, guess who is here? It's your billionaire boyfriend." Frankie grinned at Archer after calling Vera.

*****

The guards posted their selfie with Archer on the internet and it created another storm. News channels picked it up, "Archer Finch has arrived at the airport. Possibly to meet his girlfriend. Earlier there was a riot like situation at the airline desk where Vera Jones works. The airport security had to shut down the area temporarily to get the situation under control. And now billionaire Archer Finch has reached there. Could it mean another situation where people go crazy?"

Seeing the news, people who were in the lounge rushed towards the airline desk. The two guards were not able to contain the public and soon the crowd had gathered in front of the airline desk. Archer could feel how Vera must have felt with all the phone flashes in his face. But he waited patiently for her to come.

"Hey dude! She is making you wait? Seriously??" a girl yelled from the crowd. "If you were *my* boyfriend I would have never made you wait."

"Hey Archer!" another girl yelled, and as Archer looked at her, she pulled up her top and flashed her breasts to him. "Check these out! Will you be my boyfriend?"

The guys in the crowd cheered and applauded at the girl. But Archer turned back to the door, waiting for Vera.

"Sorry Man! She doesn't want to come." Frankie appeared again. "But don't you worry, we are going to get her here." He looked at the crowd and felt a little scared, "You hold on tight, eh?"

Archer saw some bright lights coming from behind. A news crew has arrived.

"Mr Finch!" the reporter was leaning over the barricade that the airport security had just laid out. "Where is Vera Jones? Are you guys still together?"

Archer remembered an old lesson by Phillip, "Never entertain the media when you are in a tense situation. It never helps!"

And this time, he decided to heed Phillip's advice. More news crews arrived and kept shooting their questions at him, but Archer maintained his focus right on that door.

And soon it happened — Archer saw Vera coming up. The moment she arrived at the gate, the whole crowd gasped. "There she is!" a girl screamed and people started cheering. The flashes of real and phone cameras filled the scene.

"See, now even I am facing this." Archer said looking at Vera. "Now we both are animals in a zoo!" Vera wanted to chuckle but she had decided to make Archer miserable for sometime. And Archer could see that Vera was in no mood for jokes.

"Listen, I was an asshole for hiding it from you. But never for a moment I thought of you as a gold digger. In fact I liked you because you laughed at me for being rich."

"What are you talking about?" Vera finally spoke.

"Remember that day when the airport was on a lock down? You and Jane were in the VIP lounge and you guys scoffed at two rich guys who took their private jet and left this airport despite the lock down?" Archer reminded her.

Vera was able to remember. Though she did not see Archer's face clearly. She instantly recalled Phillip from the lounge and the yacht. "That was you!"

"See? I like you because you hated me for being rich," Archer said.

"I did not hate you for being rich," Vera corrected him. "I was jealous of your money. People like you have always stepped over the necks of people like me. Since my childhood I saw my father being pressed by rich folks."

"You know I am not like them," Archer pleaded. "I am not like those blood suckers and you know me better than anybody present here."

Vera knew Archer was right, but she did not want to give him the satisfaction of being right. And so she remained quiet. But Archer could see that his words were working and so he continued, "Right now, I am not a billionaire. Hell, security stopped me. Ask them," Archer yelled pointing towards the security guards.

"Yeah, we did stop him," the guard told Vera.

"I am not a billionaire right now. I am just your boyfriend standing in front of you, asking for forgiveness. That's who I am right now." Archer said while going on his knees.

Seeing Archer go down, the crowd went bonkers. Cheers and applaud filled that section of the airport. A reporter extended her microphone and yelled, "Mr Finch, are you proposing to Miss Jones?"

Vera looked at Archer, "Are you?"

"Of course I am. You think I am tying my shoe laces here? I love you!" Archer defended himself.

Vera could not believe it. Her proposal was being aired live throughout the whole nation. Her mother was enjoying it as much as any other person watching it.

"Say yes!" people started cheering from the crowd.

"So??" Archer asked on his knee.

"Where is the ring?" Vera asked.

"I did not plan this through. I improvised the proposal. I don't have a ring." Archer explained. "So what it your answer. Do you want to marry me?"

"Of course I do, but…" Vera stopped in the middle of her sentence.

"But what?" Archer asked.

Vera had now started crying, "I don't know, I need to take care of my mother. I can't leave her alone."

"You don't have to. She can come live with us. Or I can come live with you. You just need to give Phillip a room. He is very peculiar about it." Archer had just solved Vera's biggest dilemma in seconds.

"Then yes! Yes I will marry you!" Vera smiled.

Archer stood up and kissed her.

The people went crazy and the news channels aired this moment live all over the nation. Archer and Vera were the new internet sensation.

Archer received a phone call from Phillip, "Congratulations Man!" Phillip said. "I just saw it on the news."

"Who would have thought, eh?" Archer replied.

Phillip then told Archer about his new plan and Archer hung up and asked Vera to come with him. "Lets go! I need to show you something."

"But I am on duty. I can't leave work!" Vera said.

Archer looked at Jane and Frankie who were standing behind Vera. In turn both of them looked at the duty manager standing behind them. The poor guy gave his approval by waving his hand.

Jane cheered and hugged Vera.

The cameras followed Archer and Vera as they left the lounge and ran onto the airstrip. People cheered and whistled on their exit. Phillip had readied the jet for them, which they boarded within a few minutes.

"We are ready for take off Mr Finch," the captain told them.

As the captain went into the flying station, Archer took Vera into the private room and locked the door from inside.

The jet took off from the airstrip and Archer held Vera in his arms. Both of them began kissing each other. Archer started taking Vera's uniform off one piece at a time. He took off her jacket and shirt, but left her scarf and skirt on. Pulling her underwear down, he placed his lips over her vagina and started sucking. Pushing his tongue inside as deep as it could go, Archer filled the jet with her loud moans. Vera kept running her fingers through Archer's beautiful golden hair and as her moans grew louder, she pulled his hair and brought his face closer to hers.

Planting a deep kiss, Vera squeezed her own breasts. Archer took a step back and looked at her. "Do that again!" he whispered and Vera used one hand to play with her breast, and the other to rub her vagina. Overwhelmed with lust, she bit her own lips and inserted her finger inside her pussy.

Archer took off his shirt and kicked his pants away after dropping them to his ankles. His stiff cock was in his hands and watching Vera made him extremely horny. Both of them enjoyed each other's bodies with their eyes and pleasured themselves for a moment.

Sitting in seats across each other Archer and Vera played with themselves and achieved a new high that they never thought was possible while touching themselves.

But now, playtime was over and they wanted to fuck each other's brains out. Archer stood up first, and grabbed Vera by her shoulders. He gently placed her over the table and spread her legs. The table was tall enough to put Vera's pussy in front of Archer's cock. Using the position, Archer slipped his dick inside Vera and held her hands behind her back. Vera could feel Archer's balls hitting her with each stroke and it drove her mad.

Her moans were growing louder but then she realized that they were not alone in the jet. To make sure that the pilots didn't hear her, she controlled herself by pressing her lips over Archer's mouth.

After some time, Vera pulled Archer towards herself and wrapped her arms around his neck. Archer knew what she wanted and so he picked her up. Planting his back against the wall, Archer held Vera in his arms and kept bobbing her up and down over his dick. Vera had locked her legs around Archer's waist to support herself.

Soon, Archer's legs started getting tired and so he sat down in a comfy seat. Vera got on her knees and started sucking his cock. She grabbed his shaft with one hand while cuddled his balls with the other. She locked her eyes with Archer while his cock was still in her mouth. Seeing Vera like this filled Archer with passion and love for this woman. He grabbed her hair and started dunking her head up and down over his cock. Archer was now controlling the speed and motion of Vera's sucking.

After thoroughly satisfying herself with Archer's cock, Vera stood up and leaned over the other seat across Archer's. She then shook her ass, inviting Archer. Her glistening pussy, was shining with the sunlight coming through the glass window. Archer stood up and positioned herself behind Vera. With one swift stroke, he was in.

Rapid thrusts, pushed Vera back and forth. She grabbed the seat to support her, while putting one of her knees on the seat. Archer held her waist with both hands, and pressing it down towards the ground, he brought it to a comfortable height.

They fucked each other in doggy style for several minutes, before Vera craved Archer's skin.

She pushed him away and sat him down in one of the seats. Mounting him like a lioness, she put his dick inside her and started ramming her from the top. Archer was feeling high and so he closed his eyes. Vera now had his broad chest and shiny skin before her. She leaned in and bit him gently on his shoulder.

Archer let out a deep moan that only increased Vera's appetite. She started moving rapidly over Archer's dick. Her nails went deep in his skin and he was grabbing her back. But as he opened his eyes, Vera's dangling breasts invited him.

He quickly put his lips around her breasts and started sucking on them. Vera was now reaching her climax. "Archer, I am about to finish!" she whispered in his ears.

Archer then wrapped his arms around her and pulled her towards him. Resting his feet on the seat opposite to him, he started thrusting his penis upwards rapidly like a jackrabbit.

And then it happened, Archer felt Vera's warm liquid gushing out over his shaft and crotch. It made him go crazy and soon he ejaculated inside her. Both of them planted kisses all over their bodies and locked each other in an unbreakable embrace.

"I love you!" Archer said to Vera. She looked into his eyes and reciprocated with a kiss.

Archer pulled a blanket from the seat behind him and wrapped it around themselves. Together, they slept like two content lovers who had no care for the world around them.

*****

Vera's eyes opened with the captain's announcement, "Mr Finch, we are ready for the landing. Please make sure you are wearing your seat-belts."

Vera looked out the window and saw nothing but water. "How is he going to land on the water?" she wondered.

Archer opened his eyes, "This one can land both on ground and water."

They quickly got dressed and got into their seats. Putting the seat belts on, they landed on the water.

"Why are we here?" Vera asked opening her seat belt.

Archer grabbed her hand and took her out to the door. The captain had opened the door for them.

Vera got out of the door and saw a small raft waiting for them. At a distance a big cruise ship was seen. Even from the distance, it was clear that the ship was having some sort of wild party.

"Come! This is what I wanted to show you." Archer took Vera's hand and they boarded the cruise. This was a festival on water. Vera had never seen a bigger party than this.

"Vera!" Alice screamed.

Vera was shocked to find her mother. Both of them hugged each other.

"I saw everything on TV!" Alice told Vera. "I am so happy for you."

Phillip appeared behind Alice and looked at Archer. Both of them shared a warm smile.

"Congratulations Mr Billionaire Boyfriend!" Phillip said with a mischievous smile.

"Thanks Man!" Archer pulled Phillip and hugged him.

"How about a picture?" a voice grabbed everybody's attention.

To Vera and Archer's surprise, Victor Cooper appeared with a camera. He took a picture and grinned at the couple, "Congratulations to you two!"

Confused, Archer looked at Phillip who explained to him why Victor was there. "The best way to kill your enemy is by making him an ally."

"And how much are we paying this ally for this?" Archer asked.

"Trust me, he doesn't know how much real professional photographers charge for a wedding like this. Besides, you saw his photos. I think he is good." Phillip said making sure nobody else heard them.

"Yeah, I liked his pictures!" Archer agreed.

"Really?" a sarcastic smile danced on Phillip's lips.

"Fuck off! I am going to stand with my girlfriend." Archer walked way from Phillip who was chuckling.

Victor came in and aimed his camera at him, "Mr Sanchez, smile!"

Phillip smiled for the camera.

Archer walked to Vera who was looking at the ocean around her.

"So, are you happy now?" Archer asked Vera.

She put her arms around Archer, "Yes! I am."

Both of them shared a kiss as Alice and Phillip watched.

"So what do you want to do now?" Archer asked Vera.

"Well today, I want to enjoy because tomorrow I have to go to work," she replied.

"You are the fiance of a billionaire. Yet you want to go and work for the cheapest airline in America?" Archer could not believe it.

"Isn't that the reason you liked me? Because I don't want your money." Vera questioned.

Archer could not think of anything, but kissing this woman. As both of them kissed, Victor slipped in and aimed his camera at them. The flash filled their faces.

Archer looked at Phillip who quietly whisked Victor away from them.

"So your mother is enjoying herself." Archer said looking at Alice who was dancing on the music.

"I guess she likes cruises." Vera wondered.

"Then how about we send her on a cruise around the world?" Archer suggested with a naughty tone.

"No, I want her to be with me." Vera punched Archer gently.

"Alright, but right now, I really want to be with you." Archer said. "And by that I mean I want to have sex with you."

Both of them smiled at each other.

"It's a big cruise ship. I guess we can find one empty room."
Vera said looking around.

She held Archer's hand and together they both disappeared
into the crowd.

The end.

If you enjoyed this ebook and want me to keep writing more,
please leave a review of it on the store where you bought it.
By doing so you'll allow me more time to write these books for
you as they'll get more exposure. So thank you. :)

Get Free Romance eBooks!

Hi there. As a special thank you for buying this book, for a limited time I want to send you some great ebooks completely
free of charge directly to your email! You can get it by going
to this page:

www.saucyromancebooks.com/physical

www.SaucyRomanceBooks.com/RomanceBooks

You can see a the cover of these books on the next page:

These ebooks are so exclusive you can't even buy them. When you download them I'll also send you updates when new books like this are available.

Again, that link is:

www.saucyromancebooks.com/physical

Now, if you enjoyed the book you just read, please leave a positive review of it where you bought it (e.g. Amazon). It'll help get it out there a lot more and mean I can continue writing these books for you. So thank you. :)

More Books By Vanessa Brown

If you enjoyed that, you'll love Her Billionaire Ex by Vanessa Brown (sample and description of what it's about below -

search 'Her Billionaire Ex by Vanessa Brown' on Amazon to get it now).

Description:

Marco was her childhood sweetheart.

That guy that showed her what love was, and the one she though she'd spend the rest of her life with.

That was, until he left her to go and live in Italy.

Now years after the sudden and unexpected leaving of her first love, Janet is a successful buyer and is doing well for her self.

Nothing can knock her off her game, or at least, nothing could until he returned!

Now a successful billionaire and head of a company in business talks with her own, she's forcefully and painfully brought face to face with the man who stole and still has her heart.

With all the heartache he's put her through, will Janet be willing to forgive and give Marco a second chance?

Want to read more? Then search 'Her Billionaire Ex Vanessa Brown' on Amazon to get it now.

Also available: Carrying His Baby by Vanessa Brown (search 'Carrying His Baby Vanessa Brown' on Amazon to get it now).

Description:

When Hallie makes manager at a high class catering company, she's over the moon.

And with her first job catering a party for the billionaire playboy Aldous, her future's looking very bright indeed.

But Aldous's party holds more surprises than she initially expected.

When a celebratory and drunken one night stand with the playboy turns into a missed period a few weeks later, Hallie soon discovers she's pregnant.

While Aldous has never been the family type, he lets her know she'll have the best care possible during her pregnancy.

But with her career taking off and the possibility of raising a child with no father figure, does Hallie even want to carry his baby?

Want to read more? Then search 'Carrying His Baby Vanessa Brown' on Amazon to get it now.

You can also see other related books by myself and other top romance authors at:

CPSIA information can be obtained at www.ICGtesting.com
Printed in the USA
LVOW10s0908030416

481969LV00019B/704/P